The Girl *in the* Picture

Rachel Hore worked in London publishing for many years before moving with her family to Norwich, where she taught publishing and creative writing at the University of East Anglia until leaving to write full time. She is married to the writer D. J. Taylor and they have three sons. Visit her at rachelhore.co.uk and connect with her on X @RachelHore and Instagram @rachel.hore.

Also by Rachel Hore

The Dream House
The Memory Garden
The Glass Painter's Daughter
A Place of Secrets
A Gathering Storm
The Silent Tide
A Week in Paris
The House on Bellevue Gardens
Last Letter Home
The Love Child
A Beautiful Spy
One Moonlit Night
The Hidden Years
The Secrets of Dragonfly Lodge
The French Spymistress

RACHEL HORE

The Girl *in the* Picture

SIMON & SCHUSTER

London · New York · Amsterdam/Antwerp · Sydney/Melbourne · Toronto · New Delhi

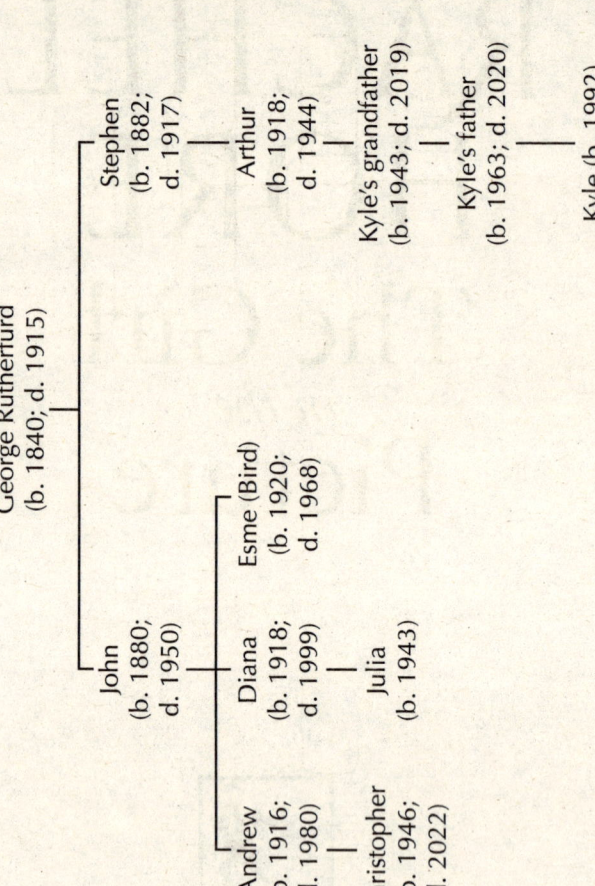

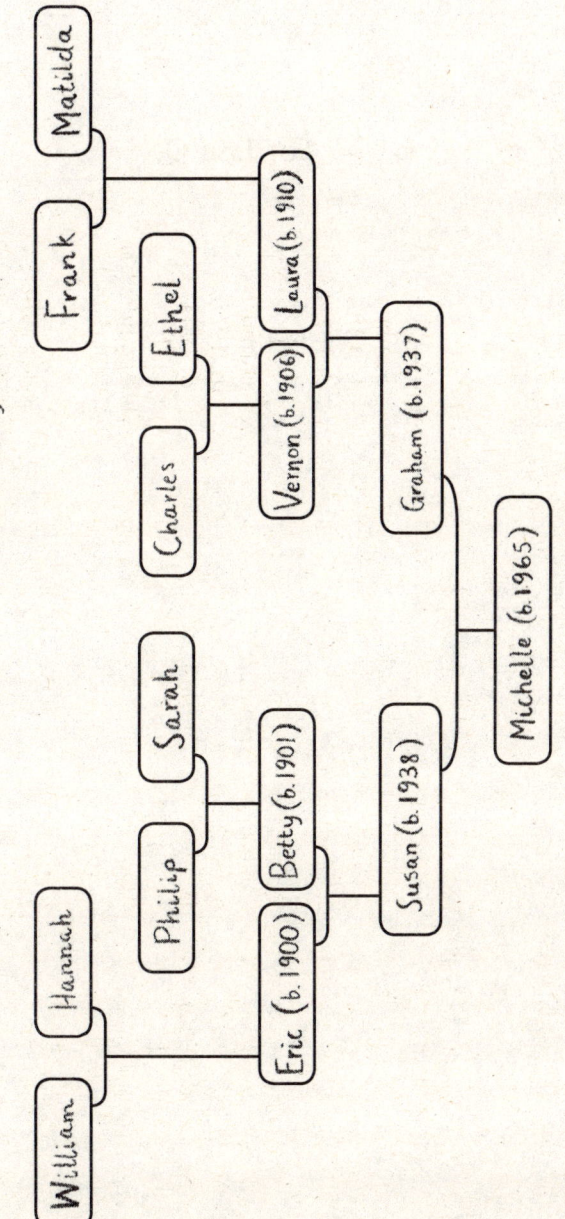

For Lisa Q.

CHAPTER 1

A House of Secrets

My heels clicked on the pavement as I followed the line of the high stone wall. I was looking for the rusty locked gate that I remembered from childhood, the gate I used to believe hid a house of secrets.

When I reached it, I stared in surprise. The iron bars, with their pattern of metal flowers, had once been battered, but now they shone with black paint. And a smart wooden sign saying 'Farthington House' had replaced the old rotten one. Things had certainly changed.

Across the road the church clock began to strike. Ten o'clock, the time of my appointment. A quick check of my phone in case of last-minute messages and I was ready.

The gate opened easily at my touch, and I did what I'd always longed to do and stepped inside. The day was sunny, but in here it was chilly. High, clipped hedges on either side cast the garden in shadow. Coils of early autumn mist rose from a dewy lawn coated with fallen leaves.

As I stood there, intrigued, the gate behind me swung shut with a clang. A blackbird flew off uttering cries of panic. A squirrel bounded with quick movements up the trunk of an oak tree. I waited as the garden settled into a watchful silence, before turning my attention to the red-brick house before me.

Its three storeys towered over the misty garden, lending it a sinister, closed-in feel. A straight gravel path ran up to a porch whose white pillars framed a forbidding black front door. I felt as if ghostly fingers from another world – a world of the past – were clutching at me. At last, I thought, with growing excitement, I might discover the secrets of Farthington House.

As a journalist on *Our Heritage* magazine, I was here to interview the house's new owner. The week before, an email from a Kyle Rutherfurd headed 'Farthington House to Open to the Public' landed in my inbox. I'd felt an immediate prickle of interest and clicked open the attached press release at once.

There had been a time when I'd known the Norfolk town of Farthington quite well. My beloved gran had lived in a nearby village and when I stayed with her as a child, we'd sometimes come in to do some shopping. On Saturdays there was a street market where I liked to spend my pocket money on sweets and cheap jewellery. The town being busy, Gran used to park in a side street a little way out. On our walk into the centre, we had to pass the intriguing rusty gate with its wonky sign.

One day, I'd hung back to peer through the bars. 'Who lives here?' I asked Gran.

'The Rutherfurd family,' Gran said briskly, not slowing her pace. 'High and mighty lot, they are. Come on, girl,' she called, marching on. 'Don't drag.'

I had to hurry to catch up.

I hadn't the courage to ask her again, though we often passed the house. Then, when I was twelve, Gran died suddenly, and I was devastated. There were no more visits to Farthington, but I always remembered the rusty gate decorated with metal flowers and wondered what secrets it hid.

Today, I hitched my bag onto my shoulder and set off up the path. But as I reached the porch, something surprising happened. The front door to the house swung inwards and a small woolly brown dog bounded out, barking. Its tail was wagging, but it still spooked me. I gasped and nearly lost my balance.

'Jess! Here!' a young man called from the doorway. Jess gave me a final yap, turned tail and ambled back inside. The man straightened. 'I'm sorry, that's not a good start,' he said, glancing at me nervously. 'Amy Collins, I think? I'm Kyle Rutherfurd.'

'Hi.' I recovered my cool. 'Don't worry, I'm usually okay with dogs.' We shook hands rather formally. He was about my age, thirty, perhaps a couple of years older, with a shy manner. Thick, cropped fair hair, clean-shaven, wearing a blue shirt that brought out the colour of his eyes. As I followed him inside, I noticed that his navy jacket was patched at the elbows. He closed the heavy door and I gazed round a dark, wood-panelled hall. The air smelled of roses, presumably from a bowl of pot-pourri next to the vase of dried flowers on a narrow table under a gilt-edged mirror.

'Jess isn't mine exactly,' he said, as we watched the dog bound away upstairs. 'She came with the house. Belongs to Aunt Julia. She came with the house, too.' His eyes crinkled at his own dry joke, then he looked at me more closely.

'It sounds complicated,' I offered. His gaze made me uncomfortable.

'Families can be complicated, don't you think?' he said gloomily 'Hey, I should say thanks for coming.'

He took my coat then opened a door situated towards the front of the hall. 'I don't know how you like to do things, but shall we sit and have a chat before I show you round?' he asked, more cheerily than before. He stood back to let me enter a formal drawing room. 'Make yourself comfortable while I grab us some coffee. Is coffee what you'd like?'

I assured him that it was and he closed the door as he left me.

I looked round with interest. The room was wood-panelled like the hall and crammed with tall bookcases and overstuffed sofas. A bright fire burned in a cast-iron grate. I wandered round, examining the pictures of countryside scenes on the walls and a collection of china statues on a shelf until Kyle returned bearing a laden tray.

'Everything's perfect!' I pointed to the vintage cups and saucers he was setting out on the coffee table. 'This room. It's like being in Victorian times.'

He beamed with pleasure. 'That's exactly the

impression I'm trying to give. My vision for this place is . . .'

'Just a moment,' I broke in, pulling out my phone. 'Do you mind if I record the interview?'

'Go ahead.'

When phone and notebook were ready, I looked up to find him watching me with that puzzled expression again.

'Sorry,' he said, embarrassed. 'It's just that you look familiar, but I can't think why. We didn't meet in London, did we? I used to work for a design agency in Covent Garden.'

I bit my lip, then shook my head. 'I'm sure I would have remembered if we had.' I had indeed worked on magazines in London before my present job and met many designers, but not Kyle.

'Odd.' He took a sip of his coffee. 'Sorry, do start.'

I thought for a second, then began the interview. 'I was so pleased to receive your email. I was always intrigued by this place,' I said, going on to tell him about my trips to Farthington as a child. 'I expect it sounds silly, but it always seemed like a house of secrets to me.' I didn't tell him what Gran had said about its owners being 'high and mighty'. That would have sounded rude.

Nor did I tell him that Amaya, my boss on *Our Heritage*, hadn't been very interested in an article about Farthington House. Her words echoed in my mind. 'No one's heard of the place. I trust you can get a good story out of your visit.' This was the reason there was no photographer with me today. I first had to write something to deserve the expense of one.

'A house of secrets!' Kyle repeated, with a dry laugh. 'Well, every family has skeletons in the cupboard, but you'd have to ask Aunt Julia about ours. I'm only a distant cousin of the Rutherfurds of Farthington House.' He finished his coffee and sat back in his chair. 'Let me explain. My several times great grandfather George built this house in 1870. He had two sons, John and Stephen, and when he died he left it to the elder boy, John, who left it to his son Andrew. Then Andrew's son Christopher had it. Christopher never married and when he died in 2022, his lawyer had to go all the way back to Stephen to trace the next male heir – me! It was a great surprise, I can tell you.'

'It had to be left to a man, not a woman?' I asked tentatively.

'That is how old George Rutherfurd set things up when he built the house and there's no evidence that Christopher tried to change it.

Christopher was a bit old-fashioned, by all accounts.'

'You mean . . . he might have left it to your Aunt Julia?' I'd never met this woman and didn't know anything about her. But I wondered how she felt about Christopher leaving Farthington House to a virtual stranger given that it was her home.

'Perhaps. But Julia – who's my distant cousin, rather than my aunt – is in her eighties. Perhaps he thought it would be too much for her. It's been quite a project doing the repairs.' Kyle glanced at his watch and stood up. 'Shall I take you round now? We can chat on the way.'

As I gathered my things he said, 'We're in the old drawing room, of course. The ceiling was grimy with soot so it had to be repainted. I bought the chairs at auction but the bookcases were already here and . . .'

Still talking, he led me back to the hall. I kept my phone recording as he took me through the ground-floor rooms. First, a grand dining room with a dozen chairs round a long table. Kyle pointed to some of the portraits on the walls. 'This is George Rutherfurd, who built the house,' he said of a severe Victorian gentleman glaring down at us. 'And here's John, his elder son, Christopher's grandfather. And John's brother Stephen, my great-great-grandfather who died in the First World War.'

'Will you have a guidebook?' I asked as I sketched a chart of the names.

'It's in preparation, but I can send you a draft.'

We moved on to a pretty sitting room at the back of the house, with a piano and more china figures in a display cabinet. A half-finished tapestry on a frame stood by the sofa. Kyle unlocked one of a pair of French doors and we stepped out onto a terrace where we stood for a moment looking out across the garden. Kyle pointed to a brick building beyond. 'That's where I live. I've converted the old stables. Part of it I use for my design work.'

I was shivering without my coat, so we went back inside. We visited a study next, filled with ancient volumes and dark leather chairs. A box of cigars lay open on the huge desk next to a letter rack. If the sitting room had felt feminine, this room felt exclusively male.

'Are there any ghosts?' I enquired, sounding brighter than I felt. I could almost sense the presence of the men who'd inhabited this room, with its faint scent of tobacco and old books.

'Not unless you count . . . no, that's unkind,' he smiled.

I wondered if he'd been going to say 'Aunt Julia' and liked the fact that he hadn't. Instead, he led me into a large kitchen where autumn daylight reflected off a rack of shiny copper pans.

The study had felt haunted; this kitchen was silent and spiritless. I gazed round at the cold cast-iron range, the scrubbed stone sinks, the empty shelves in the pantry. It was all too clean. 'It looks as though nobody's cooked anything in here for years,' I remarked.

'Christopher lived on ready meals. He had a kettle, a microwave and an old fridge. Julia has her own kitchen upstairs.'

By now I was trying to imagine the shape of my article. I'd describe the way that following the death of the elderly owner, Christopher, Kyle had carefully restored the house to its authentic Victorian state. Accurate, but a bit dry.

I wondered exactly where Aunt Julia lived, but before I could ask this, Kyle had moved on. He'd opened a door in the inner wall of the kitchen to reveal a narrow flight of wooden stairs. 'This was for the servants,' he said, standing aside. I craned my neck to see the steps wind up into darkness. 'Aunt Julia uses it, but we'll go up the grander way.'

I followed him back to the hall and up the wide, carpeted staircase to a galleried landing. Here he showed me a series of bedrooms. They were all set out in Victorian style, with patterned rugs and heavy mahogany furniture. We poked our noses into a bathroom with a huge claw-footed bath.

Next, Kyle took me past the entrance to a gloomy corridor. I glanced down it, wondering where it led, but he didn't explain.

Instead, he opened the door to a small room, which I saw was a children's nursery. There were iron safety bars on the windows, a crib and two small beds.

We stood for a moment, looking at the pattern of zoo animals on the wallpaper, a line of picture books on a low shelf. 'This is how it was,' he murmured. 'I didn't change much in here.'

He started to retreat, but I paused. Something had caught my eye. It was a small, framed painting on the wall in a dark corner. I moved closer. It was a portrait of a young woman. The size of a laptop, it glowed out of the shadows. I stepped towards it to take a better look. And behind me I heard Kyle draw a sharp breath of surprise.

'That's where I've seen you,' Kyle said, his voice full of wonder.

CHAPTER 2

A Mysterious Picture

Indeed, I saw exactly what he meant.

The girl in the picture had fair hair that was shorter than mine and wore it pinned at one side, but it was wavy like mine. Her finely painted features were mine, too. Her large blue eyes were full of fun and her small mouth looked as though she was trying not to giggle. I've seen photographs of myself with her expression.

'She does look a bit like me.' I gave a dry laugh. 'Who is she? Some long-lost relative of mine?'

He shrugged. 'I don't know, but it's an interesting idea.' He reached and unhooked the painting from the wall, then held it between us so that the light fell on it. A pendant hung round her neck in the shape of a little bluebird.

'This is the artist,' Kyle said, pointing to the letters 'T.F.' in the bottom right-hand corner.

But when he turned the painting over, there was nothing written on the torn brown backing paper. 'I found it in one of the attics,' he said, replacing it on the wall, 'and hung it here where there was an empty hook.'

We stood staring at it thoughtfully for a moment. It gave me a strange feeling. Kyle must have felt it, too, for he said, 'I know – I wonder if Aunt Julia can solve the mystery.' He lifted it off its hook again.

I hesitated, but he insisted that I accompany him. 'You'd better stop recording though,' he said, and I quickly fiddled with the phone. 'I should warn you about Aunt Julia . . . Well, she lives in the past. And she's not keen on my plans for opening the house.'

It was with a feeling of dread that I followed Kyle down the gloomy corridor that we'd passed earlier. I'd seen too many scary films in my time and Julia sounded a bit frightening. However, when he knocked on the door at the far end, the response from within was not some ghostly whisper but an elderly woman's high-pitched, 'Come in!' And when he pushed the door open, instead of finding a dark lair, I stood blinking in a splash of daylight and felt the friendly warm tongue of the little brown dog Jess licking my hand.

We had entered a large, high-ceilinged bed-sitting room situated at a corner of the house. I glanced round with pleasure. The chirps and whistles of a pair of budgies in a cage by the window were cheering. As was the fire crackling beneath a carved wooden mantelpiece. The pair of light blue fireside chairs matched the colour of the curtains and the quilt on the single bed. Through a doorway, I glimpsed a tiny modern kitchen with pot plants on a windowsill.

'Hello, Aunt Julia,' Kyle said very clearly to a slight, elderly woman, who was easing herself up from one of the chairs. 'This is Amy, who's going to write about Farthington House for a magazine. There's something we wanted to ask you.'

'You're from a magazine?' Julia peered anxiously at me through a faded version of Kyle's blue eyes. She was little, with a narrow, pointed face half hidden by untidy silver hair. 'What magazine?' Her voice quivered and she played nervously with her hands.

As I described *Our Heritage*, Julia looked more and more alarmed. I remembered Kyle's warning about her disapproving of his plans.

'Don't worry, we haven't come about that,' Kyle cut across me. 'I wanted to ask you about this.' He held up the painting of the girl. Julia reached for a pair of spectacles. As she stared at the picture, a curious expression crossed her face. She looked up at me, then back at the picture. Suddenly, she sank down in her chair again, her shoulders hunched, and stared into the fire. Sensing her mood, the dog nosed her with a gentle whine, but getting no reaction, retreated to its basket by the bed.

Kyle sat in the chair opposite Julia and leaned towards her, the portrait in his hands. 'Do you know who this is? I don't mean to upset you, but Amy is interested. Because of the likeness.'

Julia glanced at me once more with an expression of deep dismay, then seemed to come to a decision. She rose stiffly, steadied herself, then went over to a chest of drawers, on which several framed photographs were grouped around a vase of chrysanthemums. She selected one and brought it back to show us.

'This is my mother with me,' she told me with pride.

'Diana,' Kyle told me knowledgeably as I took the photograph and studied it. It was of a rather sullen-faced woman with heavy dark hair swept up in a 1940s hairdo. She was holding a shy-looking toddler in a smocked dress.

'Taken just after the war. I must have been three there.'

I didn't think Diana looked a happy mother but obviously didn't say this. I handed the photo back, wondering at its importance. Julia sat with it in her hands, lost in thought. She was not someone, it seemed, to come quickly to the point.

'Aunt Julia?' Kyle said gently.

She met Kyle's eye. Her voice, when it came, was unexpectedly sharp. 'She upset my mother greatly.'

'Who did, Julia? This girl?' He tilted the painting to show her.

'Yes,' she whispered, her distress deepening.

'Did you know her?' I asked and she shook her head. It was frustrating, like a game of twenty questions where only yes and no answers were allowed.

Kyle and I exchanged glances. He paused, then tried again. 'You know who she is or was?'

'Yes, but if anyone mentioned her name, it put Mummy in a rage. Poor Mummy. Nobody understood her except me. I knew how to calm her.'

Julia's mother must have been something of a tyrant, I thought. Or very distressed for some reason.

'Aunt Julia looked after her mother for many years, didn't you, Julia?' Kyle said brightly. He sounded out of his depth.

Julia nodded.

'When did she . . . pass away?' I enquired.

Touchingly, tears filmed Julia's eyes. 'It'll be twenty-five years next Thursday and nearly fifty years since my father left.'

I quickly calculated: 1999. 'An important anniversary for you,' I said softly and she nodded.

'I'll go to the church and light a candle for Mummy. Put flowers on her grave. She loved red roses, but there are never any roses this time of year.' She looked sharply at Kyle.

'We can find some roses, Julia,' he assured her.

'Is your father buried there, too?' I ventured.

'Oh no, they wouldn't do that.' This answer puzzled me. I imagined there had been some estrangement.

What had happened to Julia, I wondered, to make her so on edge? But we were no closer to finding the identity of the girl with the bluebird pendant. I glanced enquiringly at Kyle, who nodded slightly in reply and tried again.

'Who is this, Aunt Julia? It would be helpful to have a name.'

Julia squeezed her eyes tight and breathed in, apparently working up to an answer. 'Her name,' she said finally, 'was Bird.'

'Bird,' I echoed. The name was unusual and meant nothing to me.

'After my father left, Mummy and I moved back here with Uncle Andrew . . .'

'Christopher's father,' Kyle reminded me. 'Diana's elder brother.'

'And I heard her arguing with him about this picture. She didn't want to have to see it every day. One minute it was hanging in the dining room, the next it had gone. Where did you find it, Kyle?'

Kyle explained and she nodded.

'But who was Bird?' I persisted.

'Mummy and Uncle Andrew's little sister, of course,' Julia said.

So the girl in the portrait was definitely a Rutherfurd!

Kyle looked confused. 'I thought there were only three of them. I mean, I found a family tree Christopher drew up. His father, Andrew, your mother, Diana, and their sister Esme. John Rutherfurd's children.'

'Esme, that's right,' Julia said, brightening. 'Her real name was Esme, but everyone called her Bird.'

Kyle looked thoughtful. 'Ah,' he murmured. 'I've seen the name Esme on the family tree, but haven't able to find out anything more about her.'

'Something happened,' Julia mumbled. 'I don't know what, but Bird left. Whether she was sent away or went of her own accord, I don't know. Mummy didn't like to talk about it.'

Julia wouldn't look at us and I sensed she was hiding something.

'And now,' the old lady said abruptly, 'I've had quite enough and Jess needs to visit the garden.' We were dismissed.

Mummy didn't like to talk about it. It was these words that haunted me as we left Julia lacing her outdoor shoes and calling to her dog.

Kyle returned the portrait to its place on the nursery wall and we trooped downstairs in silence. In the hall, he turned to me. 'Aunt Julia's rather extraordinary, isn't she?'

I said politely, 'Quite a character.'

'Dominated by her mother,' he sighed. 'She can't have had much of a life, poor woman. Seems perfectly happy in her little hideaway, though.'

'Yes.' I bit my lip. 'I'm glad we've found out who the girl in the portrait is.'

'Clearly the likeness is a coincidence.'

'Of course it is.' Our families were both local, though. Perhaps there was some connection.

Just then we heard the click of a door closing

upstairs, followed by the tick of a dog's claws, then the sound of another door before silence fell once more. 'They go down the servants' stairs,' Kyle reminded me. 'Julia hates the idea of members of the public visiting the house, but I don't think she'll come across them much.'

'No,' I said.

'So. You've seen the house. What happens next?' He slid his hands into his trouser pockets and I heard the impatient clink of coins. We were back to business.

'I speak to my editor,' I said, 'and I suppose we go from there.' I saw the disappointment in his face and added hastily, 'The house is extremely interesting, I mean that.' But I badly needed to think of an approach to please Amaya. 'When are you thinking of opening?'

'Very shortly, I hope,' he said, cheering up. 'There are a lot of signs to put up and I'm still designing the guidebook, but I've been through all the legal stuff and am otherwise ready to go. I'll just need to organize publicity.'

'Of course. I'll be in touch.'

He handed me my coat and I felt sure he was watching me as I set off down the path, but when I glanced back the door was firmly closed.

Out on the street, I lent briefly against the

wall, regaining my bearings. The clock on the old church was striking twelve and a young man walked past me talking on his phone. I was back in the real world. I sighed then quickly read my messages.

Perhaps, I thought as I returned to my car, there was some story about the house's former occupants that I could work up. The most promising lead was Bird, the girl in the portrait, but Kyle didn't know much and it seemed unlikely I'd get anything more out of Julia about her. Perhaps I'd do a little research.

The fact that Bird looked like me was probably a coincidence, but the picture had made me uncomfortable. It was tangled up somehow with my childhood impression of Farthington House. It was too late to ask Gran anything, too late to ask Mum. There was only Dad left and I ought to get back to him. I started the car engine and pulled away, glad to be free of the house.

CHAPTER 3

The Bluebird Pendant

As I parked outside Dad's cottage, I was reminded that the garden hedge needed cutting. With his walking getting so bad and then the operation, he'd fallen behind with such tasks.

As ever, I felt a pang of sadness as I approached the old oak door. Mum and Dad had moved to this village from London after I'd started university in Norwich twelve years ago. For Mum it was like coming home and Dad, who ran his own small business consultancy, was a country boy at heart. Then, five years ago, Mum had been killed in a car crash after her brakes failed, and now Dad was alone. My current job was based in Cambridge where I was renting a tiny flat, but I'd been staying with Dad for a few weeks while he got over the hip replacement.

'Did the morning go well?' Dad was making sandwiches for lunch when I let myself in. He was leaning awkwardly against the kitchen worktop, his crutches to hand.

'Let me do that,' I said, rushing forward.

'I'm perfectly capable, Amy, though you can get the mayo out for me if you like.'

We ate in the living room where Dad could sit comfortably. In between mouthfuls of tuna and cucumber sandwiches, I described Farthington House and its current inhabitants. Dad didn't know the town well, but I'd told him about my fascination with the house and he'd been amused by Gran's comment that the Rutherfurds were 'high and mighty'. He had been fond of his mother-in-law, whilst sometimes falling victim to her sharp tongue.

'There was something really weird, though.' I described the painting of the girl who looked like me. 'The old lady, Julia, said she had an unusual name – Bird. That's not someone Mum or Gran ever mentioned, was it?'

Dad swallowed his mouthful then shook his head. 'Don't remember anything.'

'The artist had painted her wearing a pendant, which had a little bird on it.'

Dad looked more interested. 'What kind of bird?'

'It was blue.'

'A bluebird,' he said softly, then, after a

moment, 'Can you fetch something upstairs for me, darling? There were several boxes of things that we rescued from Gran's house after she died. Your mum always intended to sort them out, but we ended up bringing everything here. I remember her showing me some bits of jewellery tangled up in a green shoebox. Nothing valuable, but maybe . . .'

He paused, sandwich halfway to his mouth, deep in thought.

'Where are these boxes?' I said, getting up.

'Spare bedroom.' He took a bite and chewed. 'Top shelf of the cupboard,' he mumbled through his mouthful. 'Sorry, it's a bit of a mess up there.' There was no need to say what we both knew, that neither of us had the heart to go through any more of Mum's things.

Upstairs in the tiny third bedroom, I opened the cupboard to be faced with shelves packed tightly with stuff. I peeped into boxes of books and CDs, shifted bulky padded envelopes and photograph albums, telling myself to be businesslike. Many of these things had been Mum's and I couldn't bear to linger. A scrapbook with 'Life in Tudor England by Michelle Payne' in girlish felt pen on the front, a little heart instead of a dot on the 'I', made me gulp, but I hid it under a dull-looking textbook titled 'Practical Nursing' and carried on with my search.

I'd helped Dad dispose of Mum's clothes and shoes in the year after her death, taking them to a charity shop some miles away so we wouldn't risk the pain of seeing anyone local wearing them. He'd given me the few valuable items of jewellery Mum had owned and a special watercolour she'd once painted of Gran's house, Mum's childhood home. He'd have let me have more if I'd had the courage to look.

I spotted the green shoebox Dad had described at the back of the cupboard. I eased it out, undid the ribbon tied round it and peered under the lid. It contained, as he'd said, a tangle of costume jewellery, but also what looked like the contents of a dressing-table drawer – old make-up, a pin cushion, plastic combs dusted with talcum powder. What on earth did Dad want with this now and how was it connected to Bird's portrait? I shut the cupboard then carried the box downstairs.

Dad sat with the box open in his lap, unravelling the strings of dusty beads whilst I cleared a space on the coffee table. I knelt and helped him lay them out. I didn't remember Gran wearing any of them and when I said this, Dad agreed.

'She wasn't the type to wear jewellery. Maybe these were from when she was younger. There was something, though, that did come out on special occasions. Now,' he muttered to himself, 'what happened to it?'

We'd been through all the necklaces now. I leaned over the shoebox then reached in and picked out a small jeweller's box from amongst the jumble of items at the bottom. It fitted snugly in my hands as I pulled it open. Inside, lying on a velvet pad, Gran's wedding ring gleamed, the gold worn thin by years of wear. A little packet of folded tissue had been tucked next to it. I laid the box with the ring to one side, then quickly unwrapped the packet to reveal a scrap of cardboard with a silver chain wound round it. Unwinding the short chain, I realized what hung on it.

It was a little silver pendant of a bird in flight, the silver enamelled with cornflower blue.

We were both silent for a second, staring at it, then Dad whispered, 'That's the one.'

I held it up so that the bird turned slowly in the sunlight, flashing blue and silver. My mind still couldn't cope with what we'd found. I laid the pendant in my palm and studied it as calmly as I could. If this wasn't the pendant from the painting of Bird, I concluded, then it was a close copy. I fumbled with the catch and slipped the chain round my neck. The pendant rested lightly on my collarbone.

At a scraping sound, I glanced up to see Dad twisting awkwardly towards the bookcase, scrabbling at something out of reach. I scrambled up to help. 'Dad, careful.'

'Wedding photos,' he said, breathing heavily. 'Can you . . .?'

I pulled the big album from the bottom shelf, then watched him turn the thick pages, their tissue coverings fluttering, until he found the photo he was looking for. 'There.' He passed the album to me awkwardly.

It lay open at a shot of Mum and Dad, the bride and groom, standing between two sets of parents. Everyone looked so young, Mum and Dad especially, Mum radiant in a full-skirted ivory wedding dress.

Dad pointed at Gran. She was in her fifties, trim and wearing a pale blue suit. Half hidden by her blouse collar was the bluebird pendant. Perhaps I'd noticed it before – how could I have forgotten? I'd often leafed through this album as a teenager, wondering at how my fusty, middle-aged parents could ever have been so young and good-looking! How was it that Gran was wearing the same pendant as the woman in the portrait? Perhaps such pendants were more common than I thought. Bluebirds were symbols of good luck and happiness, after all. But still . . .

Suddenly I heard my phone begin to ring. I handed back the album and ran to the kitchen, where I'd left it. It was Amaya, my boss, wanting an urgent answer to a printer's query, which I was able to supply.

'Thanks,' Amaya said. 'How did you get on this morning?' She sounded rushed.

'It was interesting, but—' I started to reply.

'Put it in an email,' Amaya interrupted. 'I need to get back to the printer or we won't have a Christmas issue. Oh, and the holiday cottage piece. I'm pulling that forward to February. When can you finish it by?'

'I can start it this afternoon,' I stammered, caught off balance.

'Amazing. So I might have it by Friday?'

Today was Wednesday and it would be a fiddly article to write. Still, Amaya's word was law. 'Yes,' I sighed. 'Friday afternoon.'

The phone went dead. I glanced at the kitchen clock. Nearly two. I switched the kettle on.

'Lunch hour over,' I said crisply, returning to Dad with a mug of tea. I left him leafing sadly through his wedding album and retired to the small room by the front door that Dad normally used as an office.

I opened my laptop then watched several dozen new emails slide into my inbox. The only one that caught my interest was one from Kyle at Farthington House.

'Thank you for coming this morning,' it said. 'I'm about to Airdrop you the guidebook. If you've any useful comments, I'd be glad to hear from you. I'm better with pictures than with words, if you know what I mean!'

I touched the bluebird pendant, still round my neck, as I waited for his file to download, before clicking quickly through the pages. The brochure was beautifully designed, I saw, bright with photographs of the house, but it was thin on information about its history and the story of the Rutherfurd family. Thinking I'd need to take a more detailed look before advising Kyle, I closed the document. Then I started a new email to Amaya. I headed it 'Pitch for Article on Farthington House'.

'Farthington House,' I typed, 'has been restored as an authentic Victorian mansion. The home of the Rutherfurd family, it was built by George Rutherfurd, a local businessman from a humble background, who wanted to establish himself in society. His son John inherited both the house and the brewery George had founded. He later made his mark by becoming Mayor of Farthington.' (I had learned this from Kyle's guidebook.) 'With a social position to keep up, he and his father were responsible for commissioning many of the superb portraits of their family now displayed in the dining room of the house.'

I paused and reread what I'd written. All right but a bit dull. I tapped the desk with my fingernail, then added a few sentences about the thrill of walking round a fine Victorian house and finished by saying I was investigating the stories of the past inhabitants.

Signing off quickly, I sent it to Amaya, then turned with a gloomy sigh to a file labelled 'UK Heritage Cottages'. This was full of facts and figures that somehow had to be worked up into a sparkling piece about where readers should book next summer's holiday. I was about to set to work but found myself thinking about the email from Kyle. I should at least thank him for the morning's visit and for sending the guidebook.

I ended up writing him a detailed response, praising what he'd done to the house and suggesting very tactfully that members of the public would be interested to know more about the lives of the people who had lived there. After hitting send, I returned with a sigh to the matter of the holiday cottages and set grimly to work.

CHAPTER 4

A Family Tree

A few minutes later a sudden crash overhead followed by a yell tore me from my thoughts. 'Dad!', I cried in horror, racing upstairs.

I was relieved to find Dad sitting on the spare room bed, still holding one crutch, apparently unhurt. The cupboard door hung open and he was staring at a mess of papers spilled over the floor from a fallen box.

'Dad!' I said severely. 'What have you been doing? If you wanted something I could have fetched it for you.'

'I didn't want to disturb you.' He looked at me like a naughty puppy. 'I remembered something.' He leaned forward and poked at a pile of papers with the crutch.

I bent down and began to gather them up. They looked dull – Gran's old rent book, some gas bills. 'What were you looking for?' I asked, dumping the heap beside him on the bed.

'I'm not sure.' He began to go through the pile with feverish haste. 'It was something your mum said once about when she was a child and Gran not knowing her grandparents or not seeing them or something. I can't have been listening properly.'

'Gran didn't know who her grandparents were?' I was confused.

'Yes, when your mum was twelve, she had to make a family tree at school and that's why she'd been asking. So I thought there might be something interesting in Gran's papers.'

'Well let me know if you find anything,' I said, eyeing the time. That article would not write itself. 'Give me a shout when you're ready to go downstairs and I'll help you.' I returned to my desk and got on with my article, but at the back of my mind hung questions that needed answering.

Dad must have got himself down, because the next time I looked up from my work, it was five o'clock and outside, daylight had faded. Quickly I saved my work, replied to a couple of emails – nothing from Kyle yet – then decided I'd stop for the day. I must take something for dinner out of the freezer. I checked my phone for messages then went through to the living room. Dad was watching a quiz programme on the television but turned the sound off when I entered.

'Lasagne all right tonight?' I asked brightly, then when Dad agreed, 'Did you find anything more about Gran?'

'Nothing interesting. I'm getting better on the stairs, though.' He grinned. 'It's about planting these crutches properly, like the physio showed me, and keeping your balance.' Dad was a tall man, so I understood that this was vital.

'Gran was a woman of mystery then,' I sighed, dropping into a chair.

'It would seem so. I haven't been able to put everything away upstairs, I'm afraid.' He looked at me apologetically and I stood up again.

'I'll get it over with then,' I said, throwing him a smile. I switched on the oven, then went upstairs.

Leafing through the dry administrative details of Gran's life proved depressing. Most of this should be thrown away, I thought sadly, but I didn't have the time to sort it now and returned it to its box.

Whilst I was fitting the box back into the cupboard, I noticed the dog-eared corner of Mum's school project poking out from under the nursing textbook and a thought struck me. I set down the box then pulled out the scrapbook and turned the pages. It was mostly, as the title indicated, about life under the Tudors, but there were a couple of sets of stapled pages tucked inside on other subjects and one was the family tree project that Dad had mentioned.

I sat on the bed to look at it. There honestly wasn't much to it. The photocopied template of a family tree with space for the names of each generation had been filled in when Mum was twelve.

Mum's entry was at the bottom – 'Michelle (b. 1965)' – she'd been an only child. Above were written Gran and Grandad's names, Susan and Graham, and their two sets of parents – my great-grandparents – on the longer row above that. Gran's parents, I saw, had been called Eric and Betty. Mum had carefully written in their years of birth: Eric 1900 and Betty 1901. Since Gran was born in 1938, her entry said, they must have been considered quite old then to be first-time parents, approaching forty. I'd never met them, but Mum must have done for there were no dates of their deaths in her project. They'd have been in their late seventies at the time.

In the row above Eric and Betty, my mum had written more names: Eric and Betty's parents. Graham's parents and grandparents were there too. So what on earth had Gran meant about not knowing her grandparents? Perhaps Mum hadn't explained properly to Dad. It should be easy enough to look up a genealogy website. I'd do that later.

I turned the page and felt a tender pang at seeing a photograph of Mum at twelve. I'd always thought she looked rather like her father, Graham, with his hazel eyes and a feminine version of his nose and smile. On the next couple of pages were other photographs. Gran, wearing her hair tied back as usual, but here it was dark brown rather than the grey of later years. Her expression was fierce even then.

There were hardly any pictures of Grandad Graham's forebears, but there was a photograph of Gran's mum, Betty, a mild-looking woman in a headscarf, her coat buttoned up to her chin. It struck me I knew nothing about them beyond the fact that Eric had worked at a local brewery, and that Gran, like Mum and me, had been an only child.

The Rutherfurds of Farthington House had owned a brewery, I remembered, as I put the stapled pages to one side to show Dad. Perhaps

Eric had worked there and that was something to do with Gran referring to the Rutherfurds as 'high and mighty'. I must try to find out more.

I replaced the scrapbook in the cupboard and shut the door, then picked up the family tree. As I turned to go, I noticed a fallen envelope on the carpet, half hidden by the bedspread. I'd missed it when tidying up. I bent to retrieve it. The folded document inside turned out to be a marriage certificate. Gran and Grandad's, I realized, seeing Grandad's name, Graham Payne, and a date that sounded right – 13th April 1963. The bride's name was given as Susan Hayes – she was known as Sue – but I hadn't seen her middle name before. Ros or Rose something – the ink was blurred. I vaguely recalled Hayes as being Gran's maiden name. Grandad Graham, I'd hardly known – he'd died when I was three.

Dad put aside the book he was reading and eagerly examined the family tree. 'I love this photo of your mum,' he said wistfully. 'Eric and Betty, your gran's parents, had both passed by the time I met your mum. Apparently they lived in one of those cottages on the green near your gran and grandad.'

He was as interested as I was to see Gran and Grandad's marriage certificate. 'Rose sounds a bit too delicate for your gran.' He chuckled. 'It took me a while to get used to calling her Sue. To me, she was "Mrs Payne" until your mum and I married, and I was a bit in awe of her.'

I could imagine Gran insisting on 'Mrs Payne'. She'd been a stickler for good manners.

'Did you find her birth certificate?' I asked him, thinking it might give us more details about Gran's parents, but he shook his head.

'No birth certificate, no passport. Of course, I don't remember her ever needing a passport. Did she ever go abroad?'

I thought for a moment but didn't recall whether she ever had. They'd had no particular reason to and probably couldn't afford it. For holidays, Gran had gone to Grandad's brother and his family up in Yorkshire.

There were hints of mystery about Mum's family, but solving them was frustrating. Bluebird jewellery might have been common, but combine two appearances of a blue pendant with my likeness to the girl in the picture at Farthington House and there was surely more than coincidence at work. I felt there must be something obvious I was missing, some vital bit of information hanging just out of reach.

I sat in the study late that evening looking through free genealogy sites on the internet, but could see nothing unexpected about Gran's parents or grandparents. Eric Hayes was confirmed in a post-war census as a 'brewer's foreman' living at the address my father had mentioned, Betty as a housewife. Eventually I gave up and went to bed.

CHAPTER 5
An Afternoon at the Museum

The next morning brought replies to my emails from Amaya and Kyle. I'd just sat down to resume writing about the wretched holiday cottages and opened Amaya's message with dread. I'd been right to be anxious. 'There's not enough of a story here,' she'd written. 'The house itself sounds interesting, but our readers will want to feel some connection to the people who lived in the house. Can you find an angle here, please?' She was right, of course, and it was what I'd told Kyle was wrong with his guidebook. However, agreeing with her didn't make me feel better.

I sighed and opened the message from Kyle. I'd been half expecting a chilly response to my criticism, but instead he'd written eagerly that I'd put my finger on what was missing. 'The trouble is,' he continued, 'I don't know what happened to any family papers. The brewery didn't thrive after the war. Aunt Julia says John's son, her Uncle Andrew, lacked business sense. Farthington Brewery was sold in the 1980s, but Andrew didn't get much for it. There must be an archive about the brewery somewhere, but if Aunt Julia has any family things hidden away, she's not willing to share them. As I said, she's dead against me opening the house to public view.'

I thought for a moment, then wrote back. 'Have you consulted the online catalogues of the local museum or library? It's the obvious place to start looking for archives. And if John Rutherfurd was Mayor of Farthington, they might have some information about him.'

I didn't hear anything back immediately so closed my inbox and absorbed myself in my work, but when I checked an hour later there was an email from him. 'Good call!' he'd written. 'Nothing much online, I'm afraid, but there may be something useful on display. The museum is part of the library building and I've checked the opening times and plan to go this afternoon. You wouldn't like to meet me there, would you? There's a very swish café next door . . . We could maybe grab tea there afterwards.'

I smiled at the final sentence. I didn't really

have time to have fun but Farthington House had got under my skin. In addition, I was surprised to realize that tea with Kyle might be quite . . . nice.

The town's museum and library must have been built around the same time as Farthington House. But its high pointed roof and patterned Victorian brick were prettier, I thought, as I walked inside.

I'd agreed to meet Kyle here at two-thirty and eventually found him by the music books, leafing through a new biography of the Beatles. 'Retro tastes?' I joked.

He looked up cagily. 'Yeah. What about you?'

'Bit of a Swiftie myself.'

'Fair enough.' He slotted the book back on the shelf. 'Ready?' he said with a smile. He was dressed more informally today in jeans and a zip-up jacket and seemed more relaxed.

The museum was accessed from the library by way of an arch in the rear wall. The cheerful young woman who sat behind the museum desk glanced up from her computer screen at our approach and when Kyle told her what we were looking for, spun her wheelchair and raced away to a tall glass display case at the far side the room.

'This one's dedicated to the brewery,' she said, when we joined her. 'It was a significant employer in Farthington in its day.'

'This is where I tell you that I'm the new owner of Farthington House,' Kyle said, looking bashful.

'Oh, so you'd know all about it!'

'Well, no, that's why we're here, you see.'

'Ah!' She smiled, then turned her chair and glided off to a case by the window. 'Over here,' she called as we caught up, 'we keep the old chain the mayors wore.' We stared at it politely, then Kyle bent to examine some of the photographs displayed round it.

'I think that's John Rutherfurd,' he said, pointing to a stern-looking individual wearing the chain and apparently reading aloud from a scroll. 'The date on the label's about right, 1936. He'd have been in his fifties then.'

He asked the young woman, 'We're wondering if there are any Rutherfurd family papers in your archives. I tried looking at your online catalogue, but I couldn't see anything.'

'I'm afraid the answer's no,' she said gravely. 'We have a collection of papers about the brewery before it became part of United Ales, though. Ledgers, accounts, that sort of thing.'

'I see. Maybe not what we want. We'll have

a look round here first.' He thanked her and she returned to her desk.

I wandered back to the first display case and studied the photographs taken of the old brewery. Yet another Victorian building, it sported a long wooden sign with 'Rutherfurd Beers' painted on it. There were pictures of men in aprons rolling barrels up a ramp onto a cart, while the horse, wearing blinkers, stood patiently between the shafts. One photograph labelled 'King George V's Silver Jubilee, 1935' showed several dozen employees in suits and polished boots lined up in rows beneath a special banner. I noticed John Rutherfurd standing in the centre in his mayor's chain. I bet he never missed an opportunity to show off his position, I thought.

'What are you smiling at?' Kyle had appeared next to me.

I pointed. 'I think John Rutherfurd enjoyed being mayor,' I said.

He studied the photograph and laughed. 'He looks very self-important,' he agreed. 'Some things don't change. Honestly, some of our modern politicians! They think they're so great, then there's some scandal and they're suddenly brought down.'

'John wasn't involved in a scandal though, was he?'

'Not that I know of.'

I began to look more closely at the men in the brewery photographs, wondering if my great-grandfather Eric was one of them. There were smooth, young faces amongst their number, but you could see what they'd become after years of labour, for the oldest workers looked weathered and craggy. There were only two women, standing together at one end of a row. One looked very young, with a fresh, open expression, the other, next to her, a bit older, tired and sad-looking. I wondered at the cause of her unhappiness. For some reason, she tugged at my heartstrings.

'Things looked a bit different for the brewery in wartime.' Kyle's voice pulled me from my thoughts. He'd bent to study a photograph dated 1941. It had been taken to mark a successful scrap metal collection for the war effort. There were no young men in it. The workers standing proudly by a handcart filled with pots and pans were mostly brawny women in overalls, their hair tied up in scarves. I looked closely, but didn't recognize any as the women from the Silver Jubilee picture.

One of the men was familiar from the previous photo. Six or seven years on, he was now middle-aged and had obviously risen up the ranks, for he held a clipboard and though shortish, stood straight-backed with feet planted apart. The foreman, I guessed with a frisson of excitement. Maybe he was Eric. There was no sign of John Rutherfurd.

'What did the Rutherfurd men do in the war?' I asked Kyle.

'I did look into that,' he said thoughtfully. 'There are a couple of library books that were useful. Are we finished here?'

I nodded.

We said goodbye to the young woman on the desk, then passed back through the arch to the library. Kyle guided me to the local history section where we thumbed through some of the books. He flicked through a large illustrated book about the world wars and showed me a photograph of the Farthington Home Guard. John Rutherfurd glared from his place in the back row, next to a willowy young man, rather sickly looking. 'Andrew Rutherfurd,' I saw from the caption. John's son, then. Later in the book I spotted a 'Mrs John Rutherfurd' in a caption to a photograph featuring ladies from the Women's Institute. Socks and balaclavas they'd knitted lay displayed on a table. John's wife was a thin and nervy-looking individual with a look of her son.

'Do you think she enjoyed being Lady Mayoress?' I whispered to Kyle.

'She wasn't by that point,' he said, bending to pick out another book. 'I don't think John was mayor any more by the war years. Perhaps it was another councillor's turn.'

The book Kyle had just selected was a short memoir by a woman called Margaret Jary, but the smallness of the type and the lack of an index made it challenging to read on the spot, so Kyle borrowed it.

I was glad to step out into the fresh air and bustle of the high street, away from the clutches of Rutherfurds past who seemed to me, apart from Bird and Kyle, to be an unattractive lot.

The café next door was as swish as Kyle had described it, its Art Deco design bright with decorative mirrors and 1930s railway posters. We picked a table with comfortable padded benches, and a girl with pink hair and piercings brought us cappuccinos and almond slices, which we fell upon hungrily. Kyle watched with amusement when I scraped up milk foam with a teaspoon. His eyes lit up when he smiled.

We were back to talking about publicity. 'I'm on your side,' I explained, dabbing up the last crumbs of my almond slice, 'but my boss needs me to find a good story about the house and the family before she'll commission a piece. It's got to be more than "Man restores Victorian house and opens it to the public".'

He sighed.

I hurried on, trying to give him hope. 'If you do something like . . . invite some celebrity artist to mount an exhibition that might help, but it's stories about the people who've lived and died in the house that our readers want. We've found out a little more about your family this morning for the guidebook, but it's been mostly about the men, and John Rutherfurd in particular.' I thought for a moment then said, 'You're descended from John's younger brother Stephen, aren't you? Did the brothers get on?'

'I've no idea.' Kyle raked his fingers through his hair. 'The most exciting thing my great-great-grandfather did was to be killed in the First World War.'

The solemnity of his tone stopped me in my tracks. After a moment I said, 'I think it's the women in the family I'm most curious about. It's interesting how little you've found out about them. John's wife – do we even know her name?'

'Ann without an "e".'

'Ann,' I echoed, thinking it a modest name. 'And his daughters, Diana and Bird, the girl in the picture. Oh, Kyle, there's something I must tell you.' I fumbled in my handbag, brought out the bluebird on its chain and laid it out on the table between us.

He looked at it uncertainly, not making the connection.

'It's identical to the one in the picture, isn't it?' I prompted and his eyes widened.

'So it is. Where did you find it?' He picked up the little bird and studied it.

I told him about the wedding album and Gran's box. He agreed that bluebird jewellery must have been common.

I glanced at my watch. 'I ought to go.' I pulled on my coat as we squabbled over the bill. He won.

Outside, he said, 'How should we leave things?'

'I'm not sure.' I pointed to the library book sticking out of his jacket pocket. 'Maybe there'll be something useful in that.'

'I'll have a read and let you know,' were his last words before we parted.

My phone pinged with a message from him after supper when I was tapping away on my laptop. I paused to look. 'Remember the book I borrowed? It's fantastic. Can we meet tomorrow?'

Tomorrow was Friday. I was two-thirds of the way through the holiday cottage article and Amaya had emailed me some other tasks. Perhaps she'd give me until Monday. After all, she knew I was helping Dad. She was always going on about the importance of the work–life balance. Now was the time to test her. I phoned her quickly and she gave her assent, though I heard reluctance in her voice. 'On my desk by Monday,' she concluded, then reeled off a further list of things she wanted me to do later the following week while she took a city break to Venice.

I sighed, closed my laptop and texted back to Kyle, '3 p.m. at yours OK?' to which he quickly agreed.

CHAPTER 6

Getting to Know the Rutherfurds

I worked so quickly the following morning that I had finished the holiday cottage article by lunchtime and emailed it to Amaya, who expressed grudging thanks. After lunch, Dad asked me to collect a prescription from the doctor for some stronger painkillers, then to take it to the chemist. This took less time than I'd feared and what with one thing and another, I was twenty minutes early for my appointment with Kyle.

In case he wouldn't appreciate being interrupted in his work, I parked the car by the church, opposite the house, and had just finished dealing with a couple of text messages when the church clock chimed the quarter-hour. I glanced up at the tower, visible through the autumn trees, and, curious, got out to explore.

The wooden gate was stiff and groaned as it opened. Passing through, I found myself in a peaceful churchyard where birds sang and the long grass between the old gravestones swayed in the breeze. My feet crunched on the gravel as I followed the path up to the church porch. When I turned the iron ring in the ancient door, I found to my disappointment that it was locked.

I was about to give up when I heard a scraping noise from within, then the ring turned and the door swung inwards to reveal the stooped figure of a very old lady. 'There's a trick to the latch,' she said in a reedy voice.

I thanked her as I stepped inside and she smiled, her eyes shining like black beads in her wrinkled face. 'I'm always saying to the vicar that it puts people off, but nothing ever seems to be done about it.' She returned to the vase on a stand where she'd been arranging flowers. 'Was there anything special you wanted, dear, or are you just looking round?'

'Just looking. I have a few minutes to spare . . .'

She nodded and resumed her task. I stared round the small church. It was obviously very old, with wooden pews and lumpy stone walls, studded with memorial plaques, but it was full of light from the high windows. I set off towards the altar where a plain brass cross gleamed between two unlit candles. Above was the only source of colour, bright biblical scenes in a window of painted glass. Noah's ark was depicted in one corner of the window; I was amused by the lions' gentle faces. Gran used to take me to services in her village church, so I knew the old stories and felt comfortable here. I still loved roaming old churches, feeling a connection to the past, a sense of belonging to something that lay close, yet somehow out of reach.

I pulled myself out of my daydreams and turned my attention to the memorials, half hoping to see evidence of long-dead Rutherfurds. But amongst the marble scrolls and brass plaques recording lost fathers, mothers and young soldiers there was only one, 'Captain Stephen George Rutherfurd, aged 35, killed in action at Ypres, 20th August 1917. Beloved by all.' Kyle's great-great-grandfather. I felt a pang of sadness to see it.

The old lady was now sweeping up fallen twigs. I went to help her with the dustpan, taking the opportunity to ask, 'Are there members of the Rutherfurd family buried in the graveyard?'

'Oh yes, dear. If you turn right out of the door and go along the side of the church, you'll see a tomb with chains round it to your left. That's old George Rutherfurd and his wife. There are other graves nearby.' She looked closely at me. 'You're not a Rutherfurd yourself, are you?'

'No, no,' I said hastily. 'Just an acquaintance.' I tipped the contents of the dustpan into the woman's rubbish sack, said goodbye and managed to let myself out. The door's iron ring clunked shut.

Outside, I followed the old lady's instructions. The Rutherfurd tomb was impossible to miss among the ranks of moss-covered gravestones. It was separated from these by rusted chains, marking out the plot. I traced the inscription carved into one side. 'George John Rutherfurd, born 1840, died 1915.' So the old man had not lived long enough to have to grieve for his younger son. That had been the lot of his widow, Margaret. She'd died in 1924, the inscription informed me, and was buried here with her husband.

I tiptoed between neighbouring grave plots looking for memorials to other Rutherfurds. I found John's grave. No splendid tomb for him, only a humble square stone: '1880–1950'.

He'd outlived his younger brother Stephen by thirty-three years. The name of John's wife, Ann, had been squeezed in underneath her husband's. She'd survived until 1960, but even in death John took precedence.

What about their children, Andrew, Diana and Esme, known as Bird? I found Andrew's grave easily enough, his name carved beneath his wife Dorothy's. She'd died in 1975 and he in 1980. So their only child, Christopher, Kyle's distant cousin, was Master of Farthington House for over forty years before his death in 2022! I was just past his pristine new gravestone and found Diana's older one when, from the tower above me, three o'clock struck. With no time to explore further, I gathered my handbag from on top of George and Margaret's tomb and hurried back to the gate.

Farthington House looked a little friendlier today when I walked up the path. The front garden still lay in shadow, the house looming above, but familiarity had dispelled my fear. No ogre lived there. Kyle was friendly and kind. A sense of sadness, though, hung in the air. It spoke of secrets still to be told.

When I pressed the bell, it rang loudly inside the house, but competed with the hum of a vacuum cleaner and it was some time before anyone answered. The plump middle-aged woman who opened the door appeared to be expecting me. 'He says to go through,' she said. 'You'll find him in his studio.'

Studio was a fancy word for old stables, I thought, as I passed through the kitchen and out into the garden. I knocked on Kyle's door and hearing a 'Come in!', entered.

Looking round, I saw that 'studio' was entirely appropriate. Not a trace of the horses or their stalls remained. Instead, skylights in the sloped ceiling illuminated an airy open-plan living space with doors to other rooms set in the far side.

I hovered uncertainly on the mat. Before me was a lounge area with a squashy L-shaped sofa, the sort that you curled up and got lost in, a large glass-topped coffee table and a giant television screen fixed against a partition. To the right of this, a fridge hummed in a spacious modern kitchen and, to the far left of the room, a huge glass worktop reflected a soft white glow from three low-hanging lights. Here Kyle was sitting on a swivel chair. He was speaking to someone on his open laptop screen, but, seeing me, he quickly finished his call.

'Sorry,' I mumbled. 'The cleaner said . . .'

'No, no, don't worry, we'd done our business,' he grinned. 'Just chatting about Norwich City's chances in the league this season.'

I smiled back. 'My dad's optimistic!'

As Kyle shuffled scattered papers into a neat pile I wandered over. 'Nice,' I said, touching the smoky glass of the worktop. 'This whole place is.' I looked up at the dark grey ceiling and saw it wink with tiny stars, like the night sky.

'Good, isn't it? Practically bankrupted me, but it's the first time I've had somewhere truly my own.' A shadow briefly crossed his face. 'Thanks for coming, by the way. Take a seat.' He waved towards the sofa. 'I'll make us some tea and show you what I've found.'

I perched gingerly on the edge of the sofa whilst he prepared steaming mugs and brought them over along with the library book he'd borrowed. This he opened at a page he'd marked with a torn strip of paper. 'Margaret Jary,' he said, 'was born in a village near Farthington in 1918. It's quite a story. She was the eldest of six and the family were very poor. Her dad was an agricultural labourer but lost an arm in the First World War and couldn't get regular work. But interestingly, Margaret's mum got a job in the kitchen at Farthington House.'

He passed me the book, pointing to a chapter headed 'Farthington Brewery'. 'This page is the important one.'

I took the book from him and sipped my tea as I read. 'Ann Rutherfurd was a kindly woman,' Ms Jary had written, 'and when I was fourteen, pleaded with her husband to find me work at the brewery.'

John Rutherfurd had initially been reluctant, but Margaret was a bright girl and eventually was put to work in the brewery office under the eye of a woman named Betty Hayes. I almost dropped the book. That was my great-grandmother. I remembered the photograph in the museum with the older woman and the girl. The girl must have been Margaret and the older woman Betty!

'I see what you mean,' I breathed, then had to explain because Kyle didn't know about my great-grandparents.

'That's very interesting, but it wasn't that bit I meant,' he said. 'Read what comes next.'

So I did, with growing interest. Margaret wrote all too honestly. She didn't like her boss, John Rutherfurd, one bit. He was charming to his customers and anyone else he thought important, but behind the scenes he squeezed every effort out of his workforce and docked their wages for the smallest of faults. 'Betty Hayes's husband Eric also worked there and when Betty was ill for a few days, he asked for time off to be with her, but Rutherfurd wouldn't have it,' Margaret wrote. 'Poor Betty wasn't the same when she came back, and soon after, she left. I think that was a shame for her, but it was good for me because I got her job. That was 1938.' The year my gran was born, I thought. Was that why Betty left, because she was pregnant? Margaret didn't say.

I read on and came to the bit that must have interested Kyle. By 1938, John Rutherfurd's son Andrew was also working at the brewery. He'd been away at university, but his father wanted him in the business. 'I could see that Andrew hated the work,' Margaret wrote, 'but he wasn't given the choice. That's how things were in those days. Andrew had two younger sisters and their father bullied them, too. They were Diana and Esme, who was known as Bird. Farthington House was not a happy place. My mother said John Rutherfurd was a tyrant. Everyone had to do what he said. Bird was his favourite though.'

I turned the page, but Margaret had nothing more to say about the Rutherfurds.

'That's it,' Kyle confirmed. 'Early in 1939 she

left the brewery and went to work in the office of a factory near Norwich where they'd started to make war planes. Later she trained as a librarian then became a Labour councillor in Norwich. The book finishes in 1980 when she retires.'

'I supposed she's passed away by now,' I said, working it out. 'Or she'd be a hundred and seven! But you're right, she's given us a few clues about your family.'

'And yours, it seems!'

We looked at each other and I felt a sudden strong connection to him. Whatever the secrets of the Rutherfurd family, I was beginning to sense that they affected both of us. I told him about my own research and my visit to the church. 'Where do we look for clues next?' I wondered.

He stared at the blank TV screen and shook his head. 'I'm not sure, but after reading Margaret Jary's book yesterday, I went to confront Aunt Julia.'

'And how did that go?'

'Fairly useless.' He looked at me with a grin. 'Stubborn as a mule!'

I smiled grimly, then a thought occurred. 'Would you like me to go and try again? She might feel more at ease talking to another woman.'

'Are you sure?' His face lit up then quickly

clouded with doubt. 'She knows you're a journalist so she might not be willing.'

'I'm used to getting information out of people,' I said with more certainty than I felt.

He laughed then said in a teasing voice, 'What have you got out of me then?'

I looked round, noticing an abstract painting on the wall and a shelf of books. 'I can tell a lot from your home. You have modern tastes, but like reading history.'

'That's easy, I've just renovated a Victorian house!'

'The modern bit is a contradiction,' I smiled, easing myself more comfortably onto the sofa. 'We haven't talked about your own birth family, how you came to inherit the house.'

His smile vanished. 'My dad died suddenly a few years ago.'

A brief silence. 'I'm sorry,' I whispered. 'So did my mum.'

We could not look at one another for sadness, but I heard him swallow. Finally, he said, 'It's hard, isn't it.'

'Yup.' I brushed a piece of fluff from my jeans. We talked about our loss for a while and I was amazed at the ease of it. Dad found it very difficult to talk about Mum and always put a brave face on for the world. Kyle's mum had found a new partner and absorbed herself in a new life. He had an elder sister, who'd married and moved away with her young family.

'Dad never mentioned Farthington House,' Kyle continued. 'We had no contact with that side of the family. Stephen's son Arthur, my great-grandad, only knew his dead father as a faded photograph on the mantelpiece. Tragic, isn't it? Then Arthur himself died in battle in 1944. He was only twenty-six. So you can see how the connections were broken.'

'It was a shock then, when you were told you'd inherited this place.'

'A solicitor got in touch shortly before Christopher's death. Christopher knew he was dying, you see.' He paused briefly. 'To say I was surprised is an understatement. I was living with my girlfriend at the time in her one-bedroom flat. I was paying Sophie rent and wondering where my life was going. And all of a sudden, I was about to inherit a big house! Sophie and I discussed it endlessly, whether I should sell it, where we might live. It should have solved all my problems, but I was upset about Dad and I became pretty miserable to live with.'

'You broke up?'

He nodded. 'Christopher had died by then and once all the legal stuff was sorted out, I made the move. I'd fallen in love with the house, you see.'

'And you haven't looked back,' I said brightly.

'Yes, I have, actually. I like Farthington.' He paused. 'But it's been lonelier than I expected.'

We were silent again. I knew about loneliness. Moving from London to Cambridge had been freeing in many ways, but I hadn't yet made a network of friends there and now, of course, I was staying with Dad.

Kyle was glancing at his watch and I gathered up my things, worried I'd overstayed my welcome. 'I'll pop over and see Julia now, shall I?' I asked.

'Do you mind making your own way? I'm afraid I have another Zoom call to make. A magazine I'm designing; the client is very demanding.'

I thought about Amaya's perfectionism with *Our Heritage* and smiled. 'I'll let you know how I get on,' I promised.

As he was showing me out, he said softly, 'Hey. Thank you. I hope I haven't bored you. It's been good to talk.'

'Of course you haven't bored me!' I said, dismayed that he'd even think it. I thought we were becoming more relaxed with one another and realized with surprise that this was important to me.

CHAPTER 7

Aunt Julia Softens

'I'll be with you in a moment!' Julia had been putting away some shopping when I knocked. 'The ice cream might melt.'

'I'm sorry to have interrupted!' Jess was sniffing about my ankles, but she knew me now and quickly retreated satisfied to her basket. 'I've just been to see Kyle, but he's busy now so I thought I'd nip up and say hi.'

'You're not interrupting,' Julia said, returning to her task. A scuffling, the sound of the fridge door closing, then she came through, removed a newspaper from her chair and bid me sit in the other. 'Usually Kyle does my shopping, but he hasn't had time today. You've not come about that book he found, have you? Nasty things, that Jary woman said about the family. So unnecessary.' She glared.

'You'd seen the book before?' I asked, realizing my task would be harder than I thought.

'Someone showed it to my mother when it was published. My cousin Christopher was most put out. Wouldn't have it in the house.'

'I can see it might have been upsetting,' I said gently. 'I think Kyle's just trying to understand his family history.' I took a deep breath. 'And she wrote about my family, too.'

'What d'you mean?'

I'd got her attention now and quickly explained about Betty and Eric working at the brewery.

Her face clouded. 'I hardly remember John Rutherfurd, my grandfather. I was seven when he died, but I do recall being frightened of him. My mother used to bring me to see him and I knew instinctively he didn't understand young children. I was a nervous little girl. Once I knocked a vase of flowers off a table and he harrumphed at me. Like a camel.' She made such a funny face that I couldn't help laughing. And that made her laugh too. It made her look much younger.

'Do you remember his wife, your grandma?'

'Ann? Yes, she was the sweetest thing, but she never stood up to him. And she didn't change much after he went. Sad really.'

Her eyes softened as she thought about the past.

'Have you any more photos of the family?' I enquired carefully 'I mean, I know there are the paintings downstairs, but they're quite formal.'

Julia hesitated for only a moment. 'I suppose there's no harm,' she said to herself. She rose and went across to a glass-fronted bookcase by the window and bent to open a dark-wood cupboard at the bottom. I watched her ease out a large, leather-bound photograph album, which she brought over, sitting down with it in her lap and putting on her spectacles. Slowly, she turned the pages. It was so old that some of the photographs had come loose and she struggled to keep them in place.

She arrived at the page she wanted and angled the album towards me. I leaned to see what she was pointing at. A photograph of John Rutherfurd in his mayoral chain, scowling beneath his receding hair. Another of his wife sitting in a garden chair, a large sunhat shielding her face. A picture of Julia's mother Diana, very young in a ball gown, her square face a feminine version of her father's, the skin so smooth I knew the photo had been touched up.

I took the album from her and turned the page and my eyes widened. Here were several different shots of a young woman who was obviously Bird. She was sitting on a rug on the back lawn – I recognized Farthington House in the background – with her arm round an elderly spaniel. Her pretty smiling face and cloud of fair hair made her instantly recognizable, but here she didn't look as much like me.

'What happened to Bird?' I asked Julia, showing her the pictures with the dog.

'I never met her, you know,' Julia murmured with a frown. 'When the news came that she'd died . . .'

'She died . . . of course.' Or she'd be over a hundred now, like Margaret Jary.

'They're all dead,' Julia said wistfully. 'Mummy, Uncle Andrew, Christopher . . . I'm the only one left.'

'Apart from Kyle,' I corrected gently.

'Yes, Kyle.' Her face softened and I could see that she liked her distant cousin, even if she disapproved of his plans for the house.

'When did Bird die?' I urged.

Julia's gaze sharpened. 'I remember exactly. It was Mummy's fiftieth birthday – 1968. The news put Mummy in a rage. Said it was just like her sister to ruin her special day. That she'd ruined everything else.'

I stared at her, shocked. 'That sounds . . . I'm sorry . . . a bit harsh.'

'My mother was a very . . . bitter woman,' Julia stumbled over the words, 'but there was much good in her too. People didn't always see that.'

'What had made her so bitter?' I asked gently.

Her answer was to lean towards me and turn back a page of the album. She tapped her finger on the photograph of her grandfather John Rutherfurd and an unpleasant feeling arose in me. She said, 'Bird was his favourite child and Mummy resented that.'

I stared at the picture and saw again John's likeness to Diana. The square jaw, the determined expression. I glanced at Julia. She too could be stubborn and determined, but whoever her own father had been she'd inherited his looks rather than her mother's. I wanted to ask about who he was, but she'd stood and started fussing about, talking to her budgies as she fed them. Now wasn't the moment.

When I turned the final pages of the album, a sheet of writing paper sailed onto the floor. I picked it up and saw it was written over in biro. I found further sheets tucked untidily behind a flap inside the back cover.

Julia was still attending to her birds so I studied the paper in my hand, making out the spidery handwriting. 'It's time I set everything down,' the first phrase read, then, 'It's difficult to know where to start.' The next few words had been crossed out. Below was written the words 'Earliest Memories', then 'Who am I writing this for???' How curious.

I eased the pile of paper out from the flap and squared the pages, twenty or thirty of them, written on both sides. I flicked through, reading a name or two I recognized: 'Rutherfurd', 'Andrew', 'My sister, Esme . . .' It was a kind of personal account – it might tell me more about Bird.

Julia returned to her seat and I glanced up her enquiringly. 'I don't mean to pry, but what is this?'

Julia bent to see and an odd light came into her eyes. She reached, snatched the pages from me and held them close. 'That's private,' she said, glaring at me.

Suddenly I understood. 'Did Diana write it?'

Julia hesitated then took a deep breath. 'Mummy died in 1999, but she was housebound in her last year. She liked to rest in the sitting room and watch the birds in the garden or read or work tapestry. She grew very deaf so it was difficult to have much conversation. Instead, she started writing. I didn't know how much she'd written until after her death. She never showed me, you see. I found all this in her sewing bag. I read it, of course, but it's disturbing. I couldn't bear to see it so I put it away, but forgot where.'

'Could I read it?' I begged. 'I wouldn't do anything with it. I want to know more about Bird.'

'Why?'

'Because I look like her and . . . I don't know why exactly.'

I watched her consider my request then come to a decision. She handed the pages back to me. 'Take it. Take it away and read it.'

I stared down at the wodge of paper, my pulse quickening with excitement. I could hardly believe the trust that this stubborn old woman had just placed in me. She'd been so suspicious to begin with. How different she'd become.

'I haven't forgotten what you do for a living,' she snapped, as though she'd heard my thoughts. 'I'm trusting you to keep this to yourself.'

'You can trust me—' I began, but she broke in.

'You've a right to know.'

'A right to know,' I echoed, not understanding, but Julia hurried on.

'Yes. And Kyle thinks well of you. He can't take his eyes off you!'

I don't blush easily, but my face grew hot at that.

Watching me, she laughed and suddenly I saw that some heavy burden had been lifted from her.

'Can I show it to Kyle?'

'Read it first, then . . . maybe.' She sighed deeply, then pushed herself up from her chair, calling the dog for its walk. Our meeting was over.

I followed them down the winding backstairs and through the house to the front door.

Here I paused and got out my phone. 'I'd better tell Kyle I'm leaving,' I told her and she nodded. Jess was whining, eager to be off, so we said goodbye and the front door closed behind them. I texted Kyle asking if he still wanted me to pop back, then waited in the quiet of the hall for a response.

The cleaner had departed, but the house felt watchful. Perhaps the ghost of a uniformed maid might appear, or a whiskery gentleman in a frock coat. Instead, the only movement was a petal falling from the vase, the only sound a distant buzz of a passing motorcycle. My phone remained silent. Kyle must still be busy.

This was actually a relief. Julia had been reluctant to show him her mother's account and it felt wrong to turn up with it and not be able to tell him.

There was a further reason for my relief. A sort of shyness. Julia's comment about his interest in me had struck a tender spot. I'd been wounded by a recent rejection – a writer I'd met through work – and didn't feel brave enough to risk another just yet. I would email Kyle later, I thought, once I'd read Diana's memoir. Best to keep our relationship cool and professional.

My phone pinged and I looked at it uncertainly, but it was only Dad wondering where I was. I replied that I was coming and let myself out into the gathering darkness.

'I was worried, Amy.' I found Dad in a fretful mood and in some discomfort so I quickly handed over the painkillers.

'I was okay, Dad,' I said gently. Since what had happened to Mum, he feared the worst if someone was late. This could be annoying, but was perfectly understandable.

'The roads can be slippery this time of year. It's the leaves.' He swallowed the pills with some water and I hurried off to make dinner. He liked to eat early and I was hungry, too.

As we ate chicken stir-fry, I told him about my afternoon and about Diana's papers, still making a bulge in my handbag. I brought them out and showed them to him. He reached for his spectacles, looked at the first pages and shook his head. 'The writing's very quavery, but I'm sure you'll make it out.'

'I'd like to go through it tonight,' I said. 'Would you mind?'

'Of course not. I've a bit of admin to do myself if you'll let me use my own study.'

'I think I could allow that.' We smiled at one another. He seemed less in pain and more cheerful and naturally I was glad.

Once I'd stacked the dishwasher, I made us both coffee, fetched the handbag and my laptop and retreated upstairs. My room, under the eaves, could be chilly, but I loved the sloping ceiling, the double bed and the rosebud wallpaper I'd helped Mum choose for when I came to stay. I switched on a heater and climbed into bed, sitting with the bedside light trained on Diana's memoir, laid against my raised knees.

After the first page, Diana had continued hesitantly. For every phrase she'd let stand, another had been crossed out. I turned a couple of pages, grateful that she'd numbered them, and saw with relief that she was starting to get into her stride.

'Who am I writing this for?' I read again. This uncertain start might be tedious, but I could see her point; Julia, her own child, had seemed worried by the account and hadn't wanted to show anyone. Perhaps Diana had thought there had been no one who wanted to hear her story! If so, that was sad.

A phrase near the start of the second page startled me, though. 'The child was,' it read. What child? The next paragraph had been firmly scribbled out but then the narrative began more confidently.

'I was born on 10th November 1918, the day before the First World War ended, into a house of mourning. My Uncle Stephen had been killed the previous year, leaving his widow pregnant.' After that was more crossings out. I turned the page and read on. Diana's story had begun.

CHAPTER 8
Diana's Story

It's a terrible thing for a child to believe she isn't wanted. My mother Ann almost died giving birth to me and needed two weeks in hospital to recover. When we came home, Nurse Holden, our nanny, was given care of me. She'd been very content looking after Andrew, who was a serene two-year-old with golden hair, blue eyes and delicate features. In contrast I screamed non-stop till I was six weeks old.

Life at Farthington House revolved round my father, John Rutherfurd. When he left for work in the mornings, the household relaxed a little, but his presence remained. My mother was too meek to manage the servants properly and instead drew on his authority. 'The master will complain if we have fish again for dinner,' she'd tell Cook, or 'Mr Rutherfurd likes clean linen every day so fresh towels, please.'

When he returned from the brewery at six-thirty sharp, he expected his children to be bathed and ready for bed. We'd be led into his study to say goodnight. The room reeked of whisky and pipe smoke, and he'd ask Nurse Holden if we'd been good. 'Andrew recited his alphabet very nicely,' she'd reply, or 'He tidied the toy box,' before shaking her head over me. 'Diana spoiled her white pinafore by rolling on the grass.' Never mind that Andrew had been rolling too.

My sister, Esme, had been born two days before my second birthday. That was the first thing to blame her for. The household was too busy to remember my special day that year, and from then on, I had to share my celebrations with her.

Her reception into the family was as different to mine as could be. The stork that we were told had brought this baby must have been better at its job than the one that brought me, for my mother positively glowed with happiness when we were taken upstairs to see them after the birth. Like my brother, the baby favoured my mother, for she was delicate and pretty, with a swirl of fair hair.

Most extraordinary of all was the way my father's expression softened when he looked at her, besotted. And as she grew, my sister sensed how to charm him. She'd raise her arms to him with a gummy smile when brought to say goodnight. Mother took charge of her in a way she'd never done with me.

And a bitter seed of jealousy began to sprout inside me. I was confused. Like everyone else, I loved her. How could I not? She was sweet and pretty and charming. But at the same time, I hated her for taking all the attention. No one helped me understand my feelings and so I learned to hate myself.

It was Father who gave Esme her nickname, 'Bird'. I saw his meaning. She was slender, quick, warm and vibrant with a musical little voice. She approached life with easy charm. Strangers smiled when they looked at her. Their eyes passed over me.

Soon after his seventh birthday, Andrew was sent away to school. I missed him terribly, not least because I was left to Nurse

Holden's fuller attention. I was five and Bird three and no day passed without me attracting Nanny's displeasure. Much of it was deserved. If we painted pictures, I'd purposely knock water over Bird's efforts. I hid bits of her jigsaw puzzle, burst her balloon, tripped her up when Nurse Holden's back was turned so she'd get dirt on her dress.

A plain-faced governess, Miss de Vere, was employed for me soon after my sixth birthday. She was a kindly young woman and the individual attention helped. I responded to her interest and stopped persecuting my sister, but nothing could prevent the waves of jealousy that washed over me from time to time. Just as I knew the sky was blue, I knew that my parents loved her more than me, maybe more than Andrew, too, but Andrew was a boy and the eldest, and his place as son and heir was secure.

When she was five, Bird joined me in lessons with Miss de Vere. She had a quick mind, I could see that, but she would not sit still. Miss de Vere was enchanted and exasperated by her in equal measure. At the age of nine, I was told there would be no more lessons with my governess. I was to attend a local girls' school as a day pupil.

And thus began the happiest period of my life. The school was small, only thirty girls, aged nine to sixteen. We weren't taught very much beyond the 3Rs, history, art and a smattering of French, but I loved it all.

When I was twelve, Miss de Vere left to marry an equally plain-faced vicar so Bird joined me at school. I saw with envy how easy she was with her classmates, how the teachers indulged her, while sighing over her schoolwork. She impressed them with her artistic skills, while I was laughed at for drawing a horse that looked more like a dog.

Bird and I rarely brought friends home. I think we were both old enough to understand that our family was unlike the families of other girls. Our mother was a pale shadow, our father responsible for the house's brooding atmosphere. His moods altered wildly according to the fortunes of his business or whether a council meeting had gone his way.

It was during the spring of 1933 that the bonds tying our family together began to suffer increasing strain. I remember the time clearly because of the news. A populist bully named Herr Hitler had declared himself Chancellor of Germany and with the Great War still casting its shadow, people were concerned about peace in Europe. There was worry, too, about the high numbers of unemployed. Businesses like my father's were struggling. In the middle of this, my brother Andrew arrived home for the Easter holidays. He was seventeen by this time and up to now had obediently gone along the path our father had set out for him, which was to acquire a sound education. Predicted to gain top marks, he was expected to leave school in the summer and follow my father into the family business.

Whatever bombshell Andrew dropped in the privacy of the study, to say that my father was angry was an understatement. Raised voices reached us in the sitting room. A door slammed, my brother charged up to his room. Bird and I stared at one another in fear and puzzlement. What on earth was going on? It was our mother who eventually explained. Andrew wanted to study history at university then to follow an academic career. He would need my father to pay the fees.

In the end, it was my mother who sorted things out. Her role in the house had always been peacemaker. She would never go against my father, but she knew how to soothe him, persuade him to see points of view other than his own. It was she who'd chosen the school Bird and I attended, knowing it would suit us; she who'd ended my father's feud with the Town Clerk over some historic slight. After a fortnight of miserable argument, she suggested a compromise. Andrew went up to university in the autumn of that year, but spent his holidays working at the brewery, learning how to run the business.

For a year, family life resumed its usual rhythms, but a further storm was gathering. This time its focus was my future. In the summer after I turned sixteen, I left the school where I'd been so happy. I was aware of discussions between my parents of what to do with me but was not consulted. In August I was told I'd be moving to the seaside town of Frinton to a 'finishing school'. Here, young women from a good background were taught the skills judged necessary to catch a husband. Cookery, needlework, dancing, how to move gracefully and write a pretty thank you letter.

Nervous, I did not want to leave home and said so strongly but I was overruled.

I did not enjoy my year being 'finished'. My dancing was clumsy, my French accent terrible. The one thing I excelled at was writing. I could pen a very charming request for donations to a charitable cause. My letters home were full of lies about how much I was enjoying myself. After the summer's arguments I had no desire to upset my parents further.

Every holiday when I came home, however, something small had changed, building into something bigger that I didn't realize until it was too late. My little sister was increasingly taking centre stage.

CHAPTER 9
Diana's Story Continues

Bird was almost fifteen and, envious though I was, I could not deny that she was turning into an attractive young woman. She'd always been slender but now she was tall and willowy. Wavy fair hair fell to her shoulders, framing her large blue eyes and heart-shaped face. Her movements were graceful, her voice low and sweet. She'd hum to herself in a way I found annoying, but others loved. I tried to fight my hateful feelings, but it was difficult. If she rushed in late for dinner, my father's eyes lit up and he spoke softly. If it was me who was late, he growled. How could I not be resentful?

If I'd hoped for support from my brother, I was quickly disappointed. As agreed, Andrew spent his university holidays working at the brewery. I could see that he hated it. Having suffered our father all day, he would go to his room after dinner to study or go out with friends.

The summer after I turned seventeen, my finishing school presented the year's students with certificates of achievement and we returned home to begin adult life. Many girls were looking forward to the Season, a whirl of parties and outings designed to introduce them to suitable young men. One, an earl's daughter, was to be presented to the Queen, but our family was not important enough for that.

Still, my father was determined that I should marry well. One evening, soon after I arrived home with my bags and boxes, he requested my presence in the drawing room. I found him sitting with my mother. The day had been one of the hottest of the year and even with the windows open the room felt oppressively humid. My father stood squarely with his back to the empty fireplace and glowered at me. My mother huddled in her chair, restlessly fiddling with her pearl necklace. I perched nervously on the edge of the sofa.

'We need to discuss your future, Diana,' my father growled. 'You can't expect us to feed you for nothing, you know.' His eyes shone at his own little joke.

'I didn't expect you to,' I muttered. Where was this going? I glanced at my mother, but she only smiled.

'You need to find something to occupy you and pay your way,' my father went on. 'Until we find you a husband.'

A husband! Of course, I hoped that sometime in the dim future I would meet someone nice and fall in love. Every girl hoped that, or so I assumed. But I didn't know any attractive young men. Andrew rarely brought his friends to the house and the one or two he did were awkward, spotty and shy. There was one I felt sorry for, a local lad named Walter, who quivered every time my father spoke to him. He was the son of the Town Clerk, my father's old enemy. He and Andrew shared a love of fishing and used to go off on days together.

My father interrupted my thoughts. '. . . a teacher at Mrs Collins' school,' he was saying and I blinked. Mrs Collins ran a school for infants in her house in town and apparently needed a new assistant. I could start in September. I remember staring at him in panic. I had no interest in small children, but I knew Mrs Collins. She had a face like a currant bun and a whining voice.

'Can't I learn to type?' I stuttered, thinking an office job would be more interesting, but he shook his head.

'I'm not paying for you to waste another year. We need to have you launched, girl.'

'Launched?' For a moment I didn't understand.

'Your mother's been busy,' he said, rocking on his toes, a habit of his when excited. 'She's organizing a dance for you. In the Assembly Rooms,' he said, naming the splendid hall in town which could be hired for receptions and balls.

And finally I understood. I was to have my own season! Not a grand one in London like girls from my finishing school, but a local one for young men and women from distinguished Farthington families. My parents wished me to 'have my chance' to marry well and further the Rutherfurd fortunes!

Despite my nervousness at the idea, I was excited. Being on show would be an ordeal, but if I met a suitable man, fell in love and married him, I would both please my father and engineer my escape from my oppressive home in one fell swoop! Like most young women with a protected upbringing, I had only a fuzzy idea of life with my Mr Right, but I was determined he should be someone as different from my father as could be.

I consented to my parents' plans and was pleasantly surprised by my new life that autumn. Probably because they at last took an interest in me. My teaching duties at Mrs Collins' school were not onerous. Mrs Collins, I sensed, was overawed by my father, who was, after all, the town's mayor, and she didn't bully me as she did the other assistant.

At balls and parties, my finishing-school lessons were put to good use. I might not be a graceful dancer, but I knew the steps and how to converse with the tongue-tied young men who were my partners. They were for the most part the sons of good families, very respectable, moderately wealthy. My brother was one of them, together with some of his friends. The hapless Walter, I noticed, was not among them. Nor was my sister invited. At fifteen she was still too young even to attend my own dance. My father simply would not allow it and her complaints about this gave me a secret pleasure.

One young man caught my eye. Will Bramerton was not handsome, but I warmed to his friendly smile. He was too stocky to be a graceful dancer but off the dance floor he moved with confidence as though he knew his place in the world. He was easy to talk to and asked me about myself, which few of the other boys did, and I felt myself sparkle in his company. At every ball he picked me as his partner, which led my mother to invite him to tea. He had a car and took me out in it, showing off its speed in the country lanes. Every time we were alone together, I felt we grew closer. Of course, I was too well brought up to engage in any hanky-panky.

Perhaps in anticipation of my engagement, my father announced a special present for my eighteenth birthday. I was to have my portrait painted! He made enquiries and arranged for the chosen artist, Mr Fuller, to come to the house.

It was agreed that I should attend Fuller's studio in town every Saturday afternoon to sit for him until he was finished. I enjoyed these half-dozen sessions. Sitting perfectly still came easily to me. I would recite poetry in my head and dream of Will. And I liked Thomas Fuller, a man in his late twenties. I knew nothing about him, but he looked like my idea of an artist: dark brown hair, slightly too long, a sensitive face with full, moulded lips. His gaze might be piercing one moment and soft the next as he did his work. He only spoke when he wanted me to change position. If he had to move my head or my arm, my skin burned where he'd touched me and I blushed.

I was quite pleased with the finished picture, when Fuller brought it to Farthington House. The whole family assembled in the drawing room when he unveiled it in its gold frame and I remember the collective sigh of pleasure that went up. The deep blue ball gown I'd worn suited my dark colouring and Mother had styled my hair very prettily.

'I wish I could have my portrait painted, too,' Bird told Fuller and he smiled and glanced at my father.

'All in good time, my little Bird. All in good time,' he said.

The painting joined the other family

portraits on the wall of the dining room. I felt very proud.

On my eighteenth birthday, my parents held a party at home. After the speeches, Will took me aside and at last managed to stammer that he loved me. I was so happy that I cried. He hastened to explain, though, that his parents thought we were too young to marry. He was training to be a lawyer and not earning very much. We would have to wait several years and not announce anything yet. My tears turned to disappointment, but it couldn't be helped. At least I'd found the man I wanted to marry. I confided in my parents, who approved of Will and were content. That made me happy. I continued to teach at the school and to see Will whenever he was free.

The one irritation was Bird. She was now sixteen and it was clear she would follow the same path I had. Finishing school, a season and marriage. But where I'd been obedient, there was something restless about Bird. She was exceptionally pretty now, with large expressive eyes and a confident attitude that I envied. She could usually twist my father round her little finger, but in her last months at school they came into conflict.

That spring, Bird's abilities at art had become a passionate interest. Wherever she went she took a sketchbook. These piled up in her room. I sneaked a look once. She'd drawn bowls of fruit, children playing, sketches of her friends, and I had to admit that her work was good, very good.

Now she said she didn't want to go to finishing school. She pleaded with my father to be allowed to study art and become a painter. My father was shocked and horrified. Shocked because his favourite child was refusing to do his will. Horrified because an artist's life was hardly a respectable one. I heard him shouting, 'I forbid it,' and for once I felt sorry for her. 'You can take art lessons at finishing school,' I whispered to her and watched her eyes light up. Despite everything, I missed her in the autumn when she went away to Frinton. The house was too quiet without her humming.

It must have been November when the letter arrived from the school. I remember my father storming into the drawing room where we were waiting for Cook to call us to dinner. He demanded to speak to my mother alone and she followed him out. Andrew and I stared at each other and wondered what had happened.

We soon learned. Bird had been expelled in disgrace. My father drove off in a cloud of oily smoke to fetch her.

When she returned with all her luggage, I was concerned to see how pale and thin she was. At meals, she picked silently at her food before turning a delicate shade of green and rushing from the room. It took Cook to explain it to me. My sister was expecting a baby. Whose baby was not yet known. At first she would not say but only lay on her bed and cried. I tried my best, but it was Mother who got it out of her. By this time, rumours had started to spread.

Mrs Collins took me aside one afternoon after school. 'I hear,' she said sternly, 'that your sister is in trouble.'

I wasn't surprised that she knew – Cook was a terrible gossip – but I was shocked by what Mrs Collins revealed next. 'They're saying it's that artist, Fuller, who's responsible. Is that true?'

I remember staring at her, feeling the blood drain from my face! Thomas Fuller! For a moment my mind wouldn't process this.

But Mrs Collins was continuing. 'I think in the light of this, it would be best, Miss Rutherfurd, if you took a little break from teaching. Some of our parents can be very sensitive about these issues and I don't want anyone withdrawing their child from the school.'

I was dumbfounded. As though in a dream I collected my things and left. I don't remember the walk home.

My sister was resting when I burst into her room and confronted her. I told her what Mrs Collins had said and done and she dissolved into tears and sobbed out her story. There wasn't much to it. After Fuller's second visit to our house, when he'd brought my finished portrait and she'd begged to have hers done, he'd secretly invited her to his studio. He'd love to paint her, he said, it would be his pleasure. So she went and took her sketchbooks with her to ask his advice. Each time, after she'd sat for him, they'd talk about her drawings and discuss new techniques. And one thing had led to another.

'And I didn't know that he was m—m—married,' she cried.

I didn't want to hear the details. I felt so mixed up. Angry, filled with contempt, but also stupidly envious that Fuller had taken to my sister rather than me. Not that I wished to be in her situation, of course, taken advantage of by an older man. I would have resisted his advances, I told myself!

Later, it was anger I felt most of all, anger at the shame she brought on our family. And for everything that then went wrong for us. I blamed Bird for Will breaking off our engagement, though I knew his parents were responsible for that. There were no more invitations to dances and parties. No one would ever marry me, I believed. That's how you see things when you're only eighteen and your world falls apart. You can't think ahead to the future, that maybe things will improve. It was stupid of me to marry my brother's friend Walter, I quickly saw that, but he was the only one to ask me and I was grateful at the time. But I did not love him and treated him with contempt. Our marriage did not survive. He abandoned me to raise Julia on my own.

Poor dear Julia. I fear she's suffered from all this. I've kept her too close, trying to protect her from life. Maybe she'll read this and forgive me. As for my sister, I should have forgiven her when she was alive. It's not good to harbour grudges. But like a bird, she flew away from us, made her own life. I never thought I'd end my days back at Farthington House, but writing this has helped me. I've found a sort of peace and . . .

It was here, in the middle of a sentence, that Diana's story ended.

CHAPTER 10

What Amy Does Next

I turned the final sheet over hopefully, but there was nothing more so I tidied the pages and sat back, thinking.

My heart was full. It was clear now what had happened at Farthington House, how the fortunes of the family had declined, their lives blighted by Bird's mistake, though really, Mr Fuller should be blamed for that, being an older married man who took advantage of an innocent sixteen-year-old. But was it also John Rutherfurd's fault for his tyrannical ways? Or the fault of his own father, for impressing his ambitions on his son? Either way, John had ruled his meek wife, made sure Andrew had followed him in the family business, placed high expectations of a good marriage upon Diana and denied his beloved younger daughter the chance to follow her star.

At last, I realized, looking down at Diana's

papers, the Rutherfurd family had come to life. I understood them now – or thought I did. And I had a story, one which I knew my editor would love – not because modern readers would find it shocking or scandalous but because it would touch their hearts. But a story which, frustratingly, I might not be allowed to use. The idea of publishing it in *Our Heritage* was hugely tempting, but I did not have Julia's permission. Indeed, she'd be horrified at the idea. How could I persuade her?

I knew the best thing to do would be to consult Kyle. He had eventually texted me back earlier, but clearly still been busy. I glanced at my phone. It was after 9 p.m. now. I wondered where he'd be – out with friends, a girlfriend even. Or working or relaxing on his huge sofa in front of a film. I could at least try. I sent him a text asking him to ring me when convenient.

I waited a moment, but there was no reply, so I sighed and turned my attention to Diana's memoir once more. I had questions, many questions, but there was one that bothered me most. What exactly had happened to Bird and her baby?

It was while I was pondering this that my phone rang and seeing Kyle's name appear on the screen, I quickly answered it.

'Amy?'

'Hello, Kyle.' I could hear music faintly in the background. 'Thank you for ringing. I hope I wasn't disturbing you.'

'You're not. Is anything wrong?'

'Not exactly,' I said, then plunged in. 'You remember I went to see Julia?' I went on to explain everything that happened and gave him a brief summary of what I'd just read. 'We must ask Julia again if you can read it,' I continued. 'It's your family, after all. I understand her reluctance. Family secrets can be unsettling.'

'You're not wrong,' he laughed.

The next day would be Saturday and we both had shopping to do so we arranged to meet for morning coffee in Farthington. I would hand the memoir over to him. He would check with Julia and ask if he could read it.

After he'd rung off, I went downstairs to tell Dad everything. I could tell that he was fascinated.

'This Thomas Fuller sounds a bit of a rogue,' he said.

'I suppose he could have been unhappily married and genuinely in love with her,' I said doubtfully, 'though that's no excuse, of course.'

The thought of Fuller sent me back to my laptop and I was amazed to find a couple of lines about him in someone's blog, along with a photograph. He had indeed been dark-haired, rather Byronic-looking, I thought. I wondered idly if Bird's baby had been dark or blonde, a boy or a girl.

CHAPTER 11

The Red Suitcase

'Don't be put off by the handwriting,' I said to Kyle, sipping my cappuccino. I'd given him Diana's memoir in an envelope and he slid the pages out to glance at them.

'I'll do my best,' he said, frowning. 'Listen . . .' He paused. 'Perhaps . . .'

'Perhaps what?' I encouraged.

'Look,' he said in a rush, 'are you free tonight? I'll have the chat with Julia, then zip through this and we can talk about it over dinner.'

Dinner. It was my turn to hesitate. I wanted to accept, but I remembered what Julia had said about Kyle liking me and dinner felt intimate. Perhaps this was silly. Still, something held me back. A sort of fear of going forward. I could use Dad as an excuse – he would have to have supper on his own, though I knew he'd tell me to go out and enjoy myself. I could feel Kyle's eyes on me.

'Have I said the wrong thing? We can go out for a meal, if you like, but I propose we stay in. I'm not a bad cook, you know, and it might be easier to discuss things than in a restaurant.'

'Stay in, then,' I said, overcoming my fear. 'If you're sure. I don't want to . . .'

'I'm sure.' His eyes were warm and friendly and I felt any last resistance crumble. 'Come via the back gate – I'll leave it unlocked.'

And so it was agreed.

Later, when I let myself into Dad's cottage, his usual chair was empty. He wasn't anywhere downstairs. I stood in the hall and called out, then heard a shuffling noise upstairs. I went up to see and stared upwards in alarm. My father had pulled the loft ladder down and, leaving his crutches against the wall of the landing, had somehow climbed up it. I could just see his dimly lit figure through the open hatch, moving around.

'Dad!' I called up sharply. I was furious. 'What on earth are you doing?'

His face appeared, framed in the square hole, and he was grinning like a naughty schoolboy. 'Those new painkillers are good. And you're back just in time. Come up and take this case from me.'

I sighed crossly, but grasped the safety rail and began to climb.

Fifteen tense minutes later we were both safely seated at the kitchen table with a child's red suitcase between us. 'I suddenly remembered this was up there,' Dad explained as he wiped the dust off the case with a cloth.

'You might have waited till I got home,' I said, still upset, but he wasn't listening.

With some difficulty he managed to spring the catches on the case. It opened with a creak and a scent of dried flowers wafted out. We both peered doubtfully at the mess of papers inside.

I picked up a black and white photograph from the top. I stared at it and my heart quickened. It was of a smiling couple in their best clothes standing outside a church. The woman held a small baby wrapped in a white knitted shawl. I knew the couple's faces. I'd seen them in the pictures in Mum's project and in the ones of the brewery in the museum. I turned the photo over and read the pencilled words, 'Susan's christening, 9th April 1938.' Susan, my gran, with her parents, Eric and Betty.

I explained to Dad what I'd read in Margaret Jary's book about the woman she'd worked with at the brewery. 'It was Betty. She must have left her job suddenly because she was having a baby! A happy ending,' I said, laying the photo on the table. He watched me sift through the contents of the box. I felt I was getting close to something; I just didn't know exactly what. I picked out other photographs and studied them. Gran as a dark-haired toddler, sitting on a tricycle. One of her playing on a beach aged five or six, another as a gap-toothed schoolgirl with a gas-mask case strapped over her blazer. Here, she was a teenager sitting on a farm gate. Lovely ones of her wedding to Grandad, she radiant in a knee-length white dress.

Beneath a pile of old birthday cards, letters from a French penfriend, news clippings of Queen Elizabeth's coronation, postcards, a little autograph book, a knitting pattern, was a stiff cream envelope, slit open at the top. It was addressed to a 'Rosalie'. I frowned.

'Who's Rosalie?' I asked Dad, but he shook his head. I opened the letter and unfolded it. There were two sheets covered in handwriting, some of it clear, some of it blotched and scrawled as though the writer had lost heart. 'My darling Rosalie,' it began. I glanced at the address at the top printed in shiny black type and drew a sharp breath. Farthington House! Why had Gran got a letter addressed to a 'Rosalie' and sent from Farthington House?

Beside me, I was dimly aware of Dad reaching for his crutches, but I was too caught up in the mystery to wonder what he was doing. I turned to the final page of the letter and saw it was signed, 'Your loving mother'. While that didn't help me much, my mind was starting to make connections. Rosalie, Rose, the bluebird pendant . . .

'Dad?' I said, but Dad was stumping off into the hall and seemed not to hear me. Oh well. I turned to the beginning of the letter and began to read.

Darling Rosalie,

This is the most difficult thing I've ever written. I don't have much time. They're coming to take you from me today. You're only a week old, but I want you to know that I loved you from the first moment the nurse laid me in your arms. If I could keep you I would, but I can't. It's too hard. I'm only seventeen and I fell in love with someone I shouldn't have done and he can't marry me because he's married already. They say it's for the best and they've found a good home for you. Your new parents desperately want a baby. They will love you and look after you. You won't remember me, my darling. The pain is all mine. I will never forget you and will love you always. I don't know if you'll ever see this letter, but I'm going to ask them to give it to your new mother, whoever she is, in case she lets you read it when you're old enough. I won't blame her if she doesn't. I've had this explained to me. One other thing. I'm giving you this special pendant. Your father gave it to me as a sign of his love so I'm passing it on to you. He says bluebirds mean happiness and that I've made him happy. May it bring you happiness, too. I hope you have a marvellous life and that if you ever read this, you'll forgive me.

Your loving mother.

I sat stunned, then read the letter again, wringing the meaning from it. Baby Rosalie's mother had not supplied her own name, nor, I saw, had she dated the letter – perhaps she was too exhausted and overwhelmed to attend to such details. The mention of the bluebird pendant and the reference to the circumstances of Rosalie's birth, however, made things crystal clear. Rosalie was Bird's baby and Bird had named her.

My gran, who'd worn the pendant, was a Susan, but the name on her marriage certificate had been Rose-something. Rosalie, it had to be! Everything suddenly made sense. Gran's real mother had been Bird! And her father the artist Thomas Fuller!

Desperate for further clues, I put the letter aside and turned to the remaining items in the case: several dried roses, a cinema flyer with the film *An Affair to Remember* circled in pencil, several photographs of my mum. And at the very bottom, a long, thin brown envelope, dusty and worn. I lifted the flap and withdrew a small, folded document. It was Gran's birth certificate.

'Susan Rosalie,' it read, then gave my great-grandparents' names: Eric and Betty Hayes, 15th March 1938. My eyes widened in disbelief. If Bird was Gran's real mother, then how could it not say on a birth certificate, a legal document? But here was the name, Rosalie.

'Dad?' I took up the letter and the birth certificate and found him sitting in his chair by the fire.

'I thought I'd give you some space,' he told me.

After he'd read the letter, he looked up with a dazed expression.

'Did Mum know her mum was adopted?' I asked heavily.

He frowned and shook his head. 'She never mentioned it.'

'I wonder when Gran found out and how.' Neither of us knew the answer to that question.

We talked for some time, Dad and I, trying to work out all the links. At one point he asked me how I felt about the revelation and I said I didn't know. I hadn't taken it all in. 'I need to speak to Kyle about it,' I concluded.

It was then I remembered I was seeing Kyle for dinner and hastily explained. 'I hope you don't mind,' I said. 'I can fix your meal before I go.'

Dad grinned at me. 'Why should I mind?' he said. 'I like the idea of you having dinner with a nice young man. Bring him here sometime, I'd love to meet him.'

'Dad!' I warned sternly. 'We'll just be talking business.' Something occurred to me that should have clicked earlier and for a moment rocked me. 'I suppose he's family, isn't he?' I tried to calculate, but Dad got there first.

'From what you've told me I'd say fourth cousins.'

'Kyle and I are fourth cousins?' Family, certainly, if pretty distant, but I liked the idea of a connection to Kyle. Though I wasn't sure about being related to the other Rutherfurds.

CHAPTER 12

Dinner at Kyle's

That evening, when I let myself into the back garden of Farthington House, I felt in a peculiar way that I belonged. A warm glow from Aunt Julia's window upstairs made the house seem friendly. Soft lamps set in the wall of the stables lit the path to Kyle's door. I knocked gently and he opened the door straight away.

'Hello, you,' he smiled and stepped back to let me in.

The apartment was even more beautiful at night, with its low lighting and the stars in the ceiling twinkling, and it smelled deliciously of something savoury cooking. I curled up on the sofa with a glass of wine while Kyle went to give a pot on the hob a stir. The pages of Diana's memoir lay in a heap on the coffee table. I read the first few paragraphs again and was struck by the sadness in them.

'Did Julia let you read this?' I said when he sat down next to me.

'I coaxed her into it and read it this afternoon.' He frowned. 'So much makes sense now, but isn't it awful, how John Rutherfurd basically spoiled his family's lives.'

'I feel so sorry for them.'

'Andrew took over the brewery in the end. I wonder what happened to his dreams of teaching in a university?'

'I imagine it was the Second World War breaking out. Do you remember that picture of him in the Home Guard?' With his men from the brewery going off to fight, John Rutherfurd needed all the help he could get. Andrew, who'd looked too sickly to enrol, did his duty.

'What I want to know, is what happened to Bird in the end?'

'I know a bit more about that,' I said softly and reached in my handbag for the letter to her baby daughter.

I watched his expression change as he read it. When he came to the end, he looked up at me in astonishment and I could almost see his mind working.

'The picture,' he whispered. 'You're Bird's . . .'

'Great-granddaughter,' I finished the sentence for him. 'Bird managed to give Gran's new mother the bluebird pendant and the letter, and there must have been a time when these were passed to Gran!'

'So your gran knew she was adopted then.'

'She must have done, but Dad doesn't think she ever told Mum. This letter was right at the bottom of a suitcase of Gran's stuff so it would have been easy for Mum not to have seen it.'

'I wonder if your gran ever tried to find Bird.'

I was silent for a moment as I considered this and was about to shrug my shoulders and say no, when I remembered what Gran had said when I was a little girl and had hurried me past Farthington House. She'd said that its owners were 'high and mighty'. She'd sounded very bitter. I told Kyle this, with some embarrassment.

'I'm not surprised!' he said, unoffended. 'Though that makes me think that she knew them.'

We stared at each other, then both of us noticed a slight smell of burning and Kyle leapt up to attend to the dinner. Soon we were sitting at the dining table eating a delicious coq au vin, with dishes of chocolate mousse to follow. It was while we were lingering over the cheeseboard and chatting about our families, trying to work out who was related to whom, that we heard a knock at the door and Kyle went to open it.

To our surprise, Jess bounded in and started sniffing about. Aunt Julia hovered anxiously on the doorstep. 'Come in,' Kyle insisted and she stepped inside. 'I didn't mean to disturb you,' she said, 'but . . .'

'You're very welcome,' Kyle broke in. 'I mentioned to her that you were coming,' he told me. 'And suggested that she pop across.'

'Of course,' I said politely, wondering if there was a hidden reason.

'You've bought a new television!' Julia remarked, staring round. 'I must say, it's ridiculously large.'

I smiled to myself, thinking how out of place the elderly lady seemed in this modern setting, but Kyle quickly put her at her ease. She was soon sitting up very straight next to me on the sofa, sipping a cup of tea and discussing her mother's memoir.

When I showed her Bird's letter to the baby she gave away, she did not seem surprised.

'I suspected who you were,' she mumbled, returning it to me. 'That's really why I gave you Mummy's papers.'

'You didn't say so before,' I said surprised.

'I had no evidence, but I thought you'd work it out, too. What Bird did, the shame it brought, broke my mother, ruined her hopes. She should never have married my father; they made each other miserable. You can't imagine what it was like for me, growing up. After my father left, I was all she had and I never had the courage to leave her.'

I listened with dismay, feeling sorry for her, but I needed to know more. 'What happened to Bird?' I asked gently. 'I know when she died, but did you ever meet her?'

'No. My mother said that after Bird recovered from having the baby, she was sent to live with one of my grandmother's old schoolfriends. But she ran away. Went to London and studied art. Who paid for that, I'd like to know. Anyway, it made my mother even more bitter. Bird had got what she wanted, you see. And lived a very rackety life by all accounts.'

'As free as a bird, like her name,' I murmured, rather pleased by this idea. 'But do you really think it was her fault? Her oppressive father, an older man who seduced her . . . Things were loaded against her. And her baby was taken away.'

'I suppose you're right.' Julia sighed. 'I only ever had my mother's side of the story.'

'It's awful that Diana was so unhappy,' I said carefully, 'but what happened to Bird is no longer considered shocking. You don't need to be so secretive anymore. People will understand.'

'My mother never accepted that,' Julia said briskly.

'Did Bird every marry?' I thought to ask.

'She did and had another child, I believe.'

Another child! More family to explore. 'I wondered if Gran ever learned any of this,' I sighed. 'And what she'd have thought.'

I glanced at Julia and was alarmed to see the old lady's face crumple. Kyle and I exchanged looks of dismay and Jess pushed his doggy head into her lap. What on earth had I said to cause this?

'She came to the house once, your grandmother, Bird's daughter.' Julia whispered, clutching at Jess. 'Many years ago now. Asked for Bird. My mother had to tell her she was dead.'

I gasped. 'Gran was too late? How awful.'

'That's not the worst of it. Mummy wouldn't have anything to do with her. Sent her away. Told her never to come back.'

For a moment we all sat in silence. I was stunned. So that was why Gran had called the Rutherfurds 'high and mighty'. They'd rejected her. Poor Gran. And I finally understood quite how bitter Diana must have been.

Julia took a handkerchief from her pocket and blew her nose. 'That's it,' she croaked. 'You know everything now. It's a weight off my mind to tell you, I must say. But I've decided how to make amends.'

'To make amends?' Kyle echoed.

'Yes. You're right – the time for secrets is over. Amy, if you want to write about it all, I won't stand in your way.' She sat up straight, a red spot of emotion on each cheek and I thought she was being rather brave.

I looked at Kyle and saw he was looking at me. Agreement passed between us.

'Are you sure?' I asked her. 'It's quite a story, but I'd do it very sympathetically. After all, I'm family now. And our readers are very soft-hearted.' Although the Rutherfurds had done badly by Gran, now was the time to cast sunlight on dark corners, to explain and perhaps to forgive. And Amaya, my boss, would be delighted!

'Kyle keeps telling me the world has changed,' Julia sighed, 'but he assures me Farthington House will always be my home and that's enough. My only hope is that there will continue to be Rutherfurds living here.' There was no mistaking the meaning of the look she gave first Kyle and then me and again I felt myself blush. Really, the woman was very tactless.

She rose awkwardly, and called the dog to

her, leaving no chance for us to reply. Instead, Kyle saw her out and I joined him at the door to watch her small, upright figure cross the softly lit garden, Jess at her heels.

'Well,' Kyle said, quietly shutting the door. 'She's certainly given us our orders!'

'I'm so sorry. The cheek of . . .' I started to say, then saw his eyes crinkling with fun and we both burst out laughing.

'Dear Aunt Julia,' Kyle said, when we stopped to draw breath.

'Indeed,' I said. I noticed Diana's memoir, still on the table next to Bird's letter. 'She's left that for us, so I suppose she means what she says. You have a story for your guidebook.'

'And you have an angle for your magazine article.'

I stood silently for a moment, hugging myself, thinking. The story of the Rutherfurds had become personal. 'It's all about families, isn't it? How we learn to understand and forgive one another. I'm not sure how to tell it yet,' I explained in a wobbly voice. Suddenly, tears welled up. 'Sorry,' I said, brushing them away.

In a swift moment, Kyle was before me, his gaze tender, concerned.

'There's too much for me to take in,' I croaked. 'I keep thinking about poor Gran, finding out she's adopted, too late to find her birth mother, then being turned away by Diana. She must have felt . . . so alone.'

Gently, Kyle put his arms round me and I rested my cheek on his shoulder. He felt so strong and comforting and we stood like that for a while, gently swaying, until I recovered.

'It is a lot to take in,' he murmured in my ear, 'but there's plenty of time. You don't have to do anything you don't want to,' and I understood that in that moment something had changed between us. We truly cared about one another. I straightened in his arms and staring up at him, I saw that he'd sensed the change, too. Slowly, wonderingly, I cupped his face in my hands and our lips met in a long kiss.

There was so much to think about, to get used to. He and I must each reassess the past, embrace our new extended family and learn to trust the future, but there was something about which I felt certain. In Kyle Rutherfurd's arms, I'd come home.

ENJOYED THIS BOOK? DISCOVER MORE FROM YOUR FAVOURITE AUTHOR...

Rachel's new book, *The French Spymistress*, is available for pre-order now.

For news, event updates and information about Rachel's other books, head to **RachelHore.co.uk**

About Quick Reads

"Reading is such an important building block for success"

– Jojo Moyes

Quick Reads are short books written by bestselling authors.

Did you enjoy this Quick Read?

Tell us what you thought by filling in our short survey. Scan the QR code to go directly to the survey or visit:
bit.ly/QuickReads2026

Thank you to Penguin Random House, Hachette and all our publishing partners for their ongoing support.

A big thank you to Curtis Brown for supporting the 20th anniversary of Quick Reads.

A special thank you to Jojo Moyes for her generous donation in 2020–2022 which helped to build the future of Quick Reads.

Quick Reads is delivered by The Reading Agency, a UK charity that inspires social and personal change through the proven power of reading.

readingagency.org.uk   @readingagency   #QuickReads

The Reading Agency, Registered number: 3904882 (England & Wales)
Registered charity number: 1085443 (England & Wales)
Registered Office: 24 Bedford Row, London, WC1R 4EH
The Reading Agency is supported using public funding by
Arts Council England.

Find your next Quick Read

For 2026 we have 6 Quick Reads for you to enjoy:

Quick Reads are available to buy in paperback or ebook and to borrow from your local library. For a complete list of titles and more information on the authors and their books visit: **readingagency.org.uk/quickreads**

Continue your reading journey with The Reading Agency:

Reading Ahead

Challenge yourself to complete six reads by taking part in **Reading Ahead** at your local library, college or workplace: **readingahead.org.uk**

Book Club Hub

Join the **Book Club Hub** to find a book club and discover new recommendations: **bookclubhub.co.uk**

World Book Night

Celebrate reading on **World Book Night,** every year on 23 April: **worldbooknight.org.uk**

Summer Reading Challenge

Read with your family as part of the **Summer Reading Challeng** **summerreadingchallenge.org.uk**

For more information on our work and the power of reading visit: **readingagency.org.uk**

More from Quick Reads

If you enjoyed the 2026 Quick Reads, please explore our 6 titles from 2025:

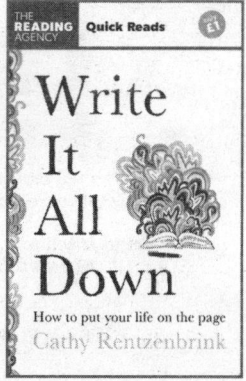

For a complete list of titles and more information on the authors and their books visit: **readingagency.org.uk/quickreads**

First published in Great Britain by Simon & Schuster UK Ltd, 2026

Copyright © Rachel Hore, 2026
Family trees by Jill Tytherleigh

The right of Rachel Hore to be identified as author of this work has been asserted in accordance with the Copyright, Designs and Patents Act, 1988.

1 3 5 7 9 10 8 6 4 2

Simon & Schuster UK Ltd, 1st Floor
222 Gray's Inn Road, London WC1X 8HB

For more than 100 years, Simon & Schuster has championed authors and the stories they create. By respecting the copyright of an author's intellectual property, you enable Simon & Schuster and the author to continue publishing exceptional books for years to come. We thank you for supporting the author's copyright by purchasing an authorised edition of this book.

No amount of this book may be reproduced or stored in any format, nor may it be uploaded to any website, database, language-learning model, or other repository, retrieval, or artificial intelligence system without express permission. All rights reserved. Enquiries may be directed to Simon & Schuster, 222 Gray's Inn Road, London WC1X 8HB or RightsMailbox@simonandschuster.co.uk

Simon & Schuster Australia, Sydney
Simon & Schuster India, New Delhi

www.simonandschuster.co.uk
www.simonandschuster.com.au
www.simonandschuster.co.in

The authorised representative in the EEA is Simon & Schuster Netherlands BV, Herculesplein 96, 3584 AA Utrecht, Netherlands. info@simonandschuster.nl

Simon & Schuster strongly believes in freedom of expression and stands against censorship in all its forms. For more information, visit BooksBelong.com

A CIP catalogue record for this book is available from the British Library

Quick Reads ISBN: 978-1-3985-5589-1
eBook ISBN: 978-1-3985-5590-7
Audio ISBN: 978-1-3985-5591-4

This book is a work of fiction. Names, characters, places and incidents are either a product of the author's imagination or are used fictitiously. Any resemblance to actual people living or dead, events or locales is entirely coincidental.

Typeset in the UK by Palimpsest Book Production Limited
Falkirk, Stirlingshire
Printed and Bound in the UK using 100% Renewable Electricity
at CPI Group (UK) Ltd